I0586141

Shunning of

Disciples

All rights reserved. No part of this publication may be reproduced, distributed, or transmitted in any form or by any means, including photocopying, recording, or other electronic or mechanical methods, without the prior written permission of the publisher, except in the case of brief quotations embodied in critical reviews and certain other noncommercial uses permitted by copyright law.

Copyright © by C. L. Conolly 2023

This is a work of fiction. Names, characters, places and incidents are either the product of the author's imagination or are used fictitiously. Any resemblance to actual persons, living or dead, businesses, companies, events or locals is entirely coincidental.

KILLER WORDS PUBLISHING
Cover art by C. L. Conolly

All rights reserved.

SHUNNING OF DISCIPLES
ISBN - 978-0-9886876-8-4

C. L. Conolly
www.clconolly.com
New Ulm, Texas

Printed in the United States of America

10 9 8 7 6 5 4 3 2 1

Shunning of Disciples

C. L. Conolly

Also written by C. L. Conolly

<u>The Affair Series</u>
Forbidden Affair
Family Affair
Fundamental Affair
Fruitful Affair

<u>Single Titles</u>
Friendly Misfortunes
Killer Suburbia

<u>Cult Series</u>
Disciples Doctrine
City of Disciples
Shunning of Disciples
Mutiny of Disciples-(early 2024)
Disbanding of Disciples-(summer 2024)

You will be shunned from the physical land, just as God will shun you from the promised land.

One

Azril reveled in all he had created as the leader of the disciples. The City of Disciples had grown over the two years it took to complete the permanent residency and medical building. Several hundred new disciples had been recruited in that time and each one of the disciples guard had participated in a connection ceremony.

Omegra, the leader's connected partner, found

out she was pregnant shortly after the permanent resident building was completed. Azril, the leader of the disciples, and Omegra were so happy to find out they were able to join the other connected partners that were expanding the disciples. Those that were born within the City of Disciples would only know how to be a disciple.

Samantha and Lawerence welcomed a little girl into the City of Disciples. Samantha may have already been pregnant when she converted as a disciple, but Lawrence accepted her and her baby.

The disciples had grown so much and there were disciples of each level throughout the City of Disciples, wearing all colors of the uniform. The three tiers had been split into groups. Cory, Danny and Martin were all tier leaders of three different tier groups.

Under each tier group leader, each disciples guard was the leader of a specific group. There were twelve groups in all, with a different disciples guard as the leader of each group. Warren, Tom, Walter, David, Jerry, Joe, Stephen, Lawerence, and Sean were all assigned as group leaders under the three tiers from Cory, Danny and Martin.

Disciples were assigned to each group in order to establish the chain of command. The disciples were to take their concerns to their group leader and if it was needed, the group leader would take that concern to their tier leader. After a discussion, if it is required, the concern would then be taken to the leader of disciples by the tier leader.

Doctor Kyle was the disciples resident doctor. He had just completed his residency in a hospital before he came to the City of Disciples. He wanted to open a private practice in a small town, but felt as though his expertise would be appreciated in the City of Disciples.

It was comforting for the disciples to know that there was a doctor within the city limits. Samantha, as well as each one of the connected partners, had prenatal care as they began procreating. Also, some of the disciples sustained injuries during their work assignments and they were able to receive medical intervention, in order to have it taken care of quickly.

The permanent resident building was also the worship building. Through the front doors was a very large foyer. To the right and the left were long hallways with rooms on both sides. Each room for the disciples was built as two bedroom, two bathroom apartments. They were equipped with a small kitchenette that consisted of a personal refrigerator, three upper cabinets and two lower cabinets with a countertop. There was a small living area for private family time.

The building was essentially shaped like a 'V'. The rooms were designed to house four disciples; two in each room. There was a hatch in the floor of the foyer where the stockpile room was located. The disciple noshery was located about two acres from the front door of the permanent residency building. There was a connecting canopy from the front door of the residency building to the noshery. The disciples assigned to cook the meals would rotate on who would retrieve items from the stock room when needed.

There was also a small stock of canned goods from the grocers that was stored in the resident rooms. It was specific for any disciples on bedrest at the request of doctor's orders. They would spend the majority of their time inside their resident room and would need a way to prepare their own sustenance.

Once the residency building had been erected on top of the buried shipping containers, a staircase was added to descend into the stock room. It was to replace the original ladder that was installed when it was pointed out as being unsafe when the disciples were carrying items up and down the ladder.

The foyer inside the resident building was set up as a common area living room for the disciples to gather and converse with each other. A set of double doors directly across from the front doors, led into the worship area. The worship area was set up to hold five thousand disciples. It wasn't just for all of the disciples that would be born within the City of Disciples, but also for the outsiders that were being converted.

Just behind the pulpit was Azril's office. Inside the office was the second hatch in the floor. It was to the left of his desk, positioned under the staircase that led upstairs to his living quarters. That hatch led down to the isolation chambers. The leader's living quarters were for Omegra, Azril and all the children God allowed them to have.

The leader's living quarters spanned the entire upstairs. The bedroom that was built for the leader and his connected partner was large enough to set up a separate area for their new baby. Once the baby was a year old, they would be moving the baby into a separate room down one of the hallways.

The hallway to the right was to be for the leader's girls and the hallway to the left was to be for the leader's boys. The hallways in the leader's quarters were set up differently than the resident rooms, but each room did get their own bathroom. Azril and Omegra, along with the disciples guard, had decided that the leader of the disciples should produce the most offspring within the City of Disciples.

When Samantha became pregnant eighteen months after her first child was born, Azril decided to make an announcement that each connected partner should only have two children at one time living in their room with them. Most disciples made the decision to have their children ten years apart, whereas others made the decision to only have two children. The leader was happy that the disciples agreed with his decision.

"What happens if we get pregnant with a third baby while already having two children living with us?" Samantha inquired.

"In the Disciples Doctrine it states, 'Each disciple who is able to give birth to a child, must be willing to incubate that child and take care of that child for no less than twenty one years. If the disciple did not choose for the seed to take hold, nor are they ready to take the responsibility of the child, it is at the discretion of the disciple as to the decision of their own body'. You are to only have two children living in your room at one time. That doesn't mean you will be shunned, or even punished for having any extra children. Omegra and I have empty rooms within our living quarters to house one of your children.

"There are plenty of common areas within the City of Disciples for you to be able to take care of your children. Just because they are sleeping in our living quarters, doesn't mean that you gave up responsibility of that child. There just isn't enough room in the disciple housing for more than four disciples. Does that make sense?" Azril explained.

"Thank you, Leader. I understand," Samantha responded.

Meals were scheduled for every disciple within the City of Disciples. Not only were the disciples on a meal schedule, but the babies as well. There were specific times in which babies and children were fed. The disciples guard ate in shifts with the different levels of the disciples.

The disciples were scheduled to eat at different times in order to avoid the fraternization of disciples amongst the different levels. It was to ensure that the highest ranking disciples in the red uniforms would eat breakfast first, then head off to their job assignments to prepare instruction for everyone else as they joined them. They were also the last to eat dinner, in order to confirm that all supplies needed for each job assignment was returned to its rightful place and organized.

The new disciples in the light blue uniforms were last to eat breakfast, out of respect for those who had established their place in the City of Disciples. They were also the first to eat dinner, so they would be the first to arrive to the worship service out of respect to the leader.

The children wearing yellow are assigned to eat at the same level as their parents. The parent is required to make sure their children have been supplied with a food tray and remain well behaved throughout their time in the noshery. All infants that require bottle feeding will be fed first, before the parents are allowed to eat.

As Omegra found disciples that would be the best fit to teach the children, she was also organizing each group from each tier to go out to recruit new disciples. Two disciples guard, along with ten disciples, were permitted to leave the City of Disciples at a time.

The rules and schedules were voted upon by the disciples to ensure inclusion in the process. Once the schedules were accepted by the disciples and the rules were agreed upon, the City of Disciples began running like a well oiled machine.

Two

Omegra produced several different pamphlets to hand out to the public. Sharon was in charge of keeping track of the inventory, as well as ordering copies of the Disciples Doctrine to sell to the outsiders. Emma kept track of the inventory on the uniforms, in order to make more if the inventory was low.

Beatrice was the only disciple who had spent

time in isolation, whereas the others in isolation had been outsiders. The shunning ceremonies were becoming few and far between. Outsiders would come into the City of Disciples after hearing the disciples share the Disciples Doctrine. Some were extremely receptive and would go out and sell all of their possessions they acquired as an outsider. When they would return, they would relinquish their funds to Azril and receive their light blue uniform.

There were a few outsiders who would come into the City of Disciples after hearing the disciples share the Disciples Doctrine and would have malicious intent. Those outsiders would be placed in isolation for seven days and given the opportunity to change their mind through private worship sessions with the leader. If they refuse, they are shunned; if they agree with the teachings as written in the Disciples Doctrine, they are given a trial period without being issued a uniform. After the trial period, they are reevaluated and either shunned, or allowed to leave with the disciples one time to sell their possessions in order to relinquish their funds to the leader and receive their light blue uniform.

Azril was sitting at his desk, in his office, when Sharon entered. The office was set up with his large executive desk facing the doors, so he could see anyone who entered. Behind him, against the wall, was an impenetrable safe with the cash funds for the City of Disciples. There were two chairs in front of his desk facing him and a loveseat against the wall next to the entrance. There was enough room for the leader, his connected partner and all twelve of the disciples guard.

With the disciples guard being at the top of the chain of command, their connected partners were treated with the same respect. Sharon was the connected partner of the disciples guard Walter.

"Beatrice wants to know when she can participate in God's cleanse, so she can receive her dark blue uniform," Sharon said.

Azril rubbed his hands against his face. "I have already had this conversation with Beatrice about this. She knows what is required of her before I will allow her to go through God's cleanse. She has not earned the right to be able to leave the City of Disciples in order to recruit the outsiders. If she is issued a dark blue uniform, she will figure out a way to get on the shuttle that leaves the City of Disciples."

Sharon leaned against one of the chairs in front of the leader's desk. "She is still trying to convince the disciples that she is your companion and she is to be treated the same as your connected partner."

Azril leaned back in his chair and crossed his arms over his chest. "Please tell me that the disciples don't believe her."

Sharon shrugged. "They usually tell her that they know she isn't because in order for the disciples to even be connected partners, they have to be on the same level. With Beatrice still being in a light blue uniform, most of them know she is lying."

"I'm tired of placing her in isolation. The last time she was isolated, she was able to be released early due to the fact that she had already been in for three months and some of the other disciples felt as though I was being unfair," Azril said.

Omegra descended the stairs from the leader's living quarters wearing an altered version of the leader's black uniform in order to make her more comfortable at eight and a half months pregnant. "I don't think isolation is working for her. Also, you never issue her cuts when she is released. Maybe you should cut her up."

Azril leaned forward, placing his elbows on the desk and his forehead on his hands. "Well that could help, but because she seems to be a loyal Disciple of God, I don't feel as though that is an acceptable response to her behavior."

"She is annoying everyone, including you. Don't deny that she hasn't pissed you off more than once," Omegra stated.

"She has also touched you inappropriately, then bragged about it to the other disciples," Sharon said.

Omegra's anger caused her to lash out in inappropriate ways. "Look, the next time she is in isolation, I'll cut her ass. I'm tired of her bullshit. Beatrice is dangerously teetering on the edge of shunning. I don't care that she was the first disciple to be recruited. She has done things since day one to try and change the message of the Disciples Doctrine."

Azril looked up and sighed heavily. "I don't have time to deal with this right now. Walter and Stephen have informed me of a few disciples planning to defect. After work detail, Cory and Danny will be bringing those disciples to my office and they will be going down into the isolation chambers. For now, Sharon bring Beatrice to me. I'll take care of her."

Sharon bowed down, kneeling on one knee in front of the leader's desk before leaving the office. Omegra sat down at one of the chairs across the desk from Azril, as soon as the door latched shut.

"How many of them do you think are going to be shunned?" Omegra asked.

"That depends upon the disciples. This is the first time we have had an issue with any of the disciples, other than Beatrice. They will have three days of isolation, along with private sermons. After those three days, the disciples then have to make the decision to stay, or they get another four days of isolation and private sermons. If they still want to defect, then they are shunned," Azril explained.

"I thought if disciples wanted to leave, they were welcome to go with only the funds they received from their disciple pay?" Omegra asked.

"If they went up the chain of command and came to speak with me about leaving, yes they would be free to go. When they are conspiring with others, that warrants either a turn around to stay in the City of Disciples and follow the Disciples Doctrine, or shunning," Azril responded.

"What if they agree to stay just to get out of isolation, but still defect anyway?"

"Everyone is free to leave whenever they want. What they are not free to do, is stage a coup to leave in a mass group. That is being sneaky and secretive and does not align with the teachings in the Disciples Doctrine. If they decide to defect alone, I will let them go. Of course, that is if they can get past the disciples guard stationed all around the perimeter of the City of Disciples."

"How many isolation chambers were built?"

"There are ten down there. They have a similar look to a prison cell, except the bathroom is closed off to give them a sense of privacy and they get their own single stall shower. They only lock from the outside and I am the only one with a key," Azril told her, exposing a chain with a key hanging around his neck.

"What would happen if you had more than ten disciples that needed to be isolated?" Omegra wondered.

"I pray to God that doesn't happen, but we have extra rooms in our living quarters that could suffice if we needed to."

"I don't think I'm comfortable with isolated disciples around our children."

"If it comes down to that, I have locks that will be installed in the room in order to keep them from escaping. The new disciples, before God's cleanse, have the right to walk out whenever they want. As for the disciples after God's cleanse, they should feel safe enough to approach either one of the disciples guard, or you, to share their concerns and hopefully we can resolve their issue. If not, they are free to leave. Like I said, they are not free to stage a coup to leave in a mass group. The first time we have more than ten disciples, or outsiders in isolation, I will request another shipping container to be buried and connected to the others with another five isolation chambers built inside."

"Okay, I understand."

Azril shifted in his chair and took a deep breath. "Work detail is almost done. I need to prepare for Cory and Danny to bring the disciples for a private sermon and possible isolation."

Omegra stood and walked around the desk. She approached the leader and kissed him on the top of his head. "I'm going to hang around for when Sharon brings Beatrice in here. You are a little too sympathetic to her pleas for leniency."

Azril positioned himself behind the desk, in order to give off the sense of authoritarian and took a few deep breaths. "Fine, but you must control yourself."

Azril heard several disciples enter the worship area, just on the other side of his office door. The disciples of each level were always doing something around the City of Disciples. After work detail, those that were scheduled to eat first were to come into the worship area for quiet reflection for five minutes before heading to the noshery. Unfortunately, the racket coming from the worship area suggested they were doing anything but quiet reflection.

Azril stood and walked over to the door of his

office. When he opened the large oak door, the sea of light blue uniforms were all gathered in the center aisle, conversing.

"Disciples, this time is to be used for *quiet* reflection. You are to file into the rows and silently recite the prayer before your meal. Please remember the teachings in the Disciples Doctrine and what is expected of you," Azril announced, from behind the leader's podium.

Once the disciples were seated and quiet, the leader returned back to his seat in his office. Omegra had moved over to the sofa and was lounging. It wasn't long before Sharon and Beatrice had arrived.

As Beatrice approached a chair in front of the leader's desk, Azril stood. "I'm so glad you wanted to see me. I feel like we haven't had a chance to have any one on one time since the last time I was in isolation."

Azril turned one of the chairs around so the back of the chair was against the front of the desk and he forced Beatrice to sit. "Beatrice, your behavior has become more and more inappropriate. You need to focus on the message in the Disciples Doctrine and stop trying to convince the other disciples that you have a higher ranking than you actually do."

Beatrice reached out and grabbed Azril's

hand. "Are you going to place me back in isolation again?"

Azril pulled his hand away and slapped her across her face. "The next time you are placed in isolation, may be the time that I decide to shun you."

"Fine. Whatever. If it wasn't for Omegra, we would be together." Beatrice swiped her hand across her cheek, as if she were trying to wipe away the sting.

Cory and Danny entered the office with six other disciples. Azril held his hand up to stop them from entering. Sharon walked over to the doors and switched places with Cory.

Azril was surprised that Omegra remained quietly seated. "Beatrice, please take tomorrow off from your job assignment and re-familiarize yourself with the Disciples Doctrine."

Cory grabbed her arm and forced her out of the office. Azril repositioned the chair Beatrice had sat in, then stepped back around behind his desk and prepared for the meeting with the defector disciples.

Three

The disciples stepped up to stand in front of Azril's desk, as Cory and Danny stood guard at the door. The leader sat down and leaned back in his chair. He shifted his eyes back and forth, trying to gauge each disciple's emotion in order to approach the situation respectfully.

Azril took a deep breath before leaning forward against his desk. "I have been made aware that there have been some rumblings about the six of you wanting to leave the City of Disciples. You could have at any point in time gone to any of the disciples guard, or even Omegra with your concerns and there could have been a respectful discussion about it. You all would have been permitted to leave. However, due to the fact that y'all felt the need to discuss sneaking out of the city, you will all be quarantined in isolation for the next three days along with participating in private sermons. Do any of you have any questions?"

"We are free to leave at any time?" Luke asked.

"Absolutely. None of you are being held against your will. Each and every one of the disciples are free to leave. I would just like to be able to talk to you first, just to be sure you made the decision all on your own and it wasn't something you were being coerced into," the leader explained.

"You mean we can just go?" Murphy asked.

"I'm sorry, but that option has passed. At this point your only option is isolation now. Cory, Danny, please join me in escorting Luke, Murphy, Heather, Skylar, Miranda and Ray down stairs to the isolation chambers," Azril requested.

The leader lifted the hatch in the floor under the staircase that led up to his living quarters. He was the first to descend the stairs as the others followed behind. Each isolation chamber was marked with a number on the door. Next to each door, hanging on the wall between each room, was a clip board. Azril wrote down the name of the disciple as each one was placed in separate rooms. Cory and Danny headed back upstairs.

Azril used the key that hung around his neck to lock the doors once the disciples were settled in. He walked over to the wall next to the stairs and lifted a microphone that had been hung to communicate with those in isolation. The microphone was linked to speakers in each room.

"I will return after the sermon to speak with each of you. Just keep in mind, this is a private space for reflection. There is a copy of the Disciples Doctrine in each one of your rooms. Please feel free to read through the Disciples Doctrine and find a prayer that you feel pertains to your current circumstance." The leader then replaced the microphone to its holder and ascended the stairs, closing the hatch once he had stepped up into the office.

He walked over to the desk and picked up his sermon notes. Cory and Danny were standing near the doorway to the office. As Azril walked toward the door, Cory pushed it open, then stepped aside in order for the leader to exit first.

The worship center was full and a few stragglers were heading in.

As the leader of the disciples stepped up to the podium, the disciples guard that were lined up at the front of the worship area, watching the disciples enter for worship, took their seats with their connected partners. Cory and Danny stepped up to their posts at each end of the stage, and Omegra was already seated behind and to the right of Azril for support.

"As we welcome new disciples into the City of Disciples, please understand that none of you are being held against your will. You are free to leave at any time. I just ask that you please approach the disciples guard who is the head of the tier you have been assigned to in order to set up a meeting with me, so we can discuss your concerns with staying in the City of Disciples.

"My connected partner, Omegra, is also available to talk. The discussion will only address your concerns and we will never try to manipulate you into staying here against your will. You chose to come here and you have the choice to leave. What I don't want you to do, is trying to stage a mass escape with other disciples. If you want to leave, that's fine, but don't try to convince others that your negative feelings are their feelings as well and you should all try to escape.

"The City of Disciples is here for positive rein-forcement. If you feel negatively about being here, please don't feel as though you need to escape as if you live in a prison. God instructed me to build the City of Disciples as a safe place for any-one to worship the greatness that God has given us here in the physical land without having to wor-ry about the negativity that is all around us in the outside world. If we worship what God has given us in the physical land, He will welcome us in the promised land.

"Let us pray for strength. God, give us the strength that we need to get through this difficult time. We need strength in order to trust the leader of the physical land is showing us the way into the promised land. We need strength to follow Your teachings in order to make it into the promised land. Some days we may feel like we are falling away. Other days we feel like we are following You. Please, God, give us the strength that we need to follow Your teachings as told by the leader of the physical land. We are Disciples of God and we will appease You in worship.

"Thank you for joining me tonight. I understand that this may have been a little bit of a different sermon, but after some information was brought to my attention, I want to make sure that each and every one of you understands that you are not being held against your will. I will be in my office for the next few hours for anyone who would like to talk. Cory and Danny will take your names, then bring the list to me. I will call you in one at a time and you can tell me how you feel. I appreciate each and every one of you as disciples and hope that you feel safe here." Azril bowed his head, before turning and heading back into his office.

Four

Luckily there were only three disciples that wanted to discuss their place within the City of Disciples and they were fairly new. None of them had been through God's cleanse yet, so they were still searching for purpose. Azril was able to reassure them that God had a purpose for them in the physical land and gave them some passages to read from the Disciples Doctrine.

Once he was finished speaking with the new disciples, the leader headed down to the isolation chambers. Stopping at the first door, Azril picked up the clipboard. Disciple Luke was the name written on the page. He unlocked the door, slowly turned the knob and entered the room. Luke was laying on the bed and reading the Disciples Doctrine.

"Disciple Luke, have you found any passages that you may have questions about?" Azril asked.

Luke sat up and made eye contact with the leader. "No, I just want to leave. I don't understand why we are being held prisoner down here. Just let us go."

Azril was confused, because Luke was wearing an orange uniform. "You already had the option to leave, but as soon as you began plotting a mass escape, that's when you broke the rules of the City of Disciples. Now we will decide if you want to stay, or if you are going to be shunned from the physical land. You have been here for a while already and have made it to level two. Why would you want to leave?"

Luke rolled his eyes, as he crossed his arms over his chest. "Whatever, just shun me now. I would rather die than be stuck here for three days."

"I'm genuinely curious. Why do you want to

leave the City of Disciples? Have we not been good to you? Are you not feeling fulfilled?" Azril wondered. "I really want to know. Tell me what you were doing before you were recruited."

"I was homeless, living on the streets. I thought I would have a better life here because I would have a warm bed to sleep in, I was able to shower daily and knew where and when my meals were coming. At this point, I would just rather be homeless. I hate all the work that I have to do here. That's the exact reason why I was homeless; it's because I hate working," Luke replied.

The leader wanted to try to compromise with the disciple. "If you have a problem with your work detail, we can change it, so you can do something that you would rather do."

Luke shook his head. "Nope. I don't want to work at all. I want to be able to do whatever I want and go wherever I want at any time. If I could just be shunned, at least I know I will be free. I just don't understand why I have to spend three days locked up, when all I want to do is leave."

"Everyone gets a fair chance to change. I will make sure you get a dinner tray and I will be back in the morning to check on you," Azril told him, then left the room and locked the door.

The leader wrote on the page that was attached to the clipboard that Luke was unwilling to compromise and follow the rules of the City of Disciples. As he placed the clipboard back on the wall, Cory was walking down the stairs.

"Azril, we have a bit of an issue. Several outsiders breached the main gate. The disciples guard has them contained for now, but where would you like us to take them?" Cory informed.

Azril continued with the isolated disciples and stepped up to room two. "Do you know why they chose to breach the City of Disciples?"

Cory shook his head. "No sir. We just grabbed them and detained them."

The leader nodded and took a deep breath. "Okay, for now just cuff their hands behind their backs, lead them into the worship area and have them all kneel in the shunning area. I will be up as soon as I am done here."

Cory bowed his head, then ascended the stairs as the leader unlocked the door to the second room. He picked up the clipboard and saw that Disciple Skylar was in that room. She had been with the disciples since they had moved onto the new property. As he opened the door and stepped inside, the disciple was kneeling next to the bed reciting prayers from the Disciples Doctrine.

Skylar looked up as the leader stepped inside.

"Hello, Leader."

"I'm sorry to disturb you during prayer," Azril told her, when she stood up.

Skylar placed her hands, palms together, in the center of her chest. "You didn't disturb me. I'm glad to see you. I would just like to let you know that Luke and Murphy were the ones who were talking about leaving the City of Disciples. The rest of us were just caught talking to them when they were overheard discussing their plan to escape. I can assure you that they are the only two wanting to leave. I love it here and feel safe in the City of Disciples. Please Leader, I don't want to be shunned."

"If you are sure you want to stay, then you are free from isolation and you can go back to your room. I will be sure you have a dinner tray delivered to you," Azril reassured her, then held the door open for her to leave.

The disciple knelt down in front of him for blessing. "Thank you so much, oh great leader of disciples."

She headed down the hall toward the staircase. Azril followed behind her to be sure that she wouldn't be hassled on her way out. Just as he reached the top of the stairs, he remembered the outsiders who were being held hostage just outside of the office.

The leader placed a hand on her shoulder to stop her from leaving the office. "Skylar, let me get one of the disciples guard to escort you back to your room. I don't want them to think you escaped."

Skylar nodded. "That might be a good idea. Do you want me to wait here?"

Azril lowered the hatch door and locked it. "Yes, just stay here and I will be right back."

He walked over and slipped through the door that led out to the worship center, only cracking it open enough for him to slip through, as she took a seat at one of the chairs in front of his desk. There were four outsiders on their knees in the shunning area. Each one was handcuffed and gagged. All twelve of the disciples guard were standing in front of the outsiders, as Azril approached Cory about the disciple.

"I have Skylar in my office. She is dedicated and states that Luke and Murphy were the only ones discussing leaving. Do you know anything about that?" Azril asked Cory.

Walter held his hand up with one finger pointing to the ceiling to interject. "Luke and Murphy were discussing leaving with the others."

The leader focused his gaze on Walter. "But you never heard the others agreeing with them?"

Walter shrugged. "All six of them were standing around in a group. Stephen and I heard Luke and Murphy talking about leaving. The two of them sounded as though they were making a plan with the other four. That's when we brought it to your attention."

Azril rubbed his mouth and sighed heavily. "Okay, well now I have Skylar in my office waiting to be escorted to her room and I still have three other disciples in isolation that now need to be released because you jumped to conclusions. Next time this happens, tell Cory, Danny, or Omegra, so one of them can speak to each disciple individually and let them determine the status of the disciples before jumping to conclusions and assuming they all need to be isolated. Now, I need the outsiders hidden before she comes out of there. I don't want to alarm the disciples as to the presence of a possible threat."

Cory nodded. "No problem. We got you. As soon as we move them, I will come in there and get her to escort her back to her room. By then you may have talked to the others and may have more to take back."

"Thank you, Cory." The leader turned his focus to his other trusted disciples guard. "Martin, can you go into my office and stay with Skylar until the other disciples guard can get rid of the outsiders for now?"

"Yes sir," Martin told him, heading into the office.

Azril nodded to the rest of the disciples guard and headed into the office with Martin. The leader sat down in the chair next to the disciple.

Azril vaguely explained the situation to Skylar. "Cory will be in to get you in a few moments. We had a situation that needed my instruction and the rest of the disciples guard are taking care of that right now to make sure that you make it to your room safely."

Skylar placed her hands on her cheeks. "Thank you, Leader. I appreciate your love and attention to the safety of the disciples."

Azril reached over and grabbed one of her hands. "I still need to go downstairs and get Ray, Miranda and Heather, but first, I want to know what made you choose to live in the City of Disciples."

Skylar lowered her head, as if she was ashamed of what she was going to tell him. "There was ten of us that had decided to go out one night. We all went to a bar to go drinking and I had a little too much to drink. A couple of my friends tried to help me get home, but because I was so intoxicated I could barely walk, they eventually just left me on the sidewalk.

"I had vomited on myself and eventually a

strange man was trying to undress me. That was when a car was passing by. It stopped and someone got out. When the man realized he had been caught, he ran off. The person who had exited the vehicle, helped me into the passenger seat and cleaned me off."

Tears were streaming down her face. Azril reached up and swiped her cheek with his thumb. "We have all made mistakes in the past. If you learn from them and change, it makes you a better person. Please, continue."

Skylar blinked slowly, before continuing. "I passed out on the ride and woke up in one of the disciple's rooms. It was Emma. She was so sweet and took care of me for a couple of days, reading the Disciples Doctrine to me and bringing me to the worship services. I felt safe and happy here and that was when I decided I wanted to stay."

Azril stood and placed his hand on top of her head for a blessing, proud of her strength. "I am so happy you are here. Thank you so much for sharing with me."

He walked back over to the hatch under the stairs. The leader unlocked the hatch and opened it, slowly descending down to the isolation chambers. Azril was intrigued to speak with the other isolated disciples.

Five

Azril stepped up to the third room, picked up the clipboard and read the name. Ray was in room three. The leader unlocked the door and saw Ray sitting on the bed, legs crossed, with his hands on his knees. He appeared to be praying, so the leader waited.

Ray slowly opened his eyes, then turned his head to look at the leader. "I'm so glad to see you,

Leader. None of us were given a chance to speak to the disciples guard who overheard Luke and Murphy talking to us about escaping. Luke and Murphy want to leave, the rest of us don't."

Azril nodded and walked over to sit on the bed next to the disciple. "I understand. I spoke with Skylar and she told me the same thing. I just want to make sure the rest of you feel the same way she does. First, I want to know what made you choose to live in the City of Disciples."

Ray looked down at the floor, took a deep breath and began. "Last year my wife and I were expecting our first baby. We had been married for two years, but together for five. I felt like I had met my soul mate. When she went into labor, she was only thirty weeks pregnant and she thought we were going to lose the baby. She said the pain seemed like something was wrong, so I rushed her to the hospital. As soon as I had opened the car door to get her inside, the pain became so unbearable for her and she passed out. I had to flag down a nurse to bring out a wheelchair in order to get both my wife and my baby taken care of.

"They rushed her in to delivery for an emergency c-section. She had apparently had a blood clot that had formed in the umbilical cord. Something called umbilical artery thrombosis. My wife was already having issues with preeclampsia. The pain and stress that something was wrong with the baby caused her to go into ventricular tachycardia due to an undiagnosed heart issue that she had apparently had since she was a kid. I lost them both that day."

Azril reached up and placed his hand on Ray's back. "That must have been so hard for you. I can't imagine the emotional tole that had on you."

Ray had tears welling in his eyes. "I was so lost and didn't know what I was going to do with myself. When I left the hospital, I just started walking down the road. I was thinking about taking my own life when I came across a large group of people listening to someone teach them about the disciples. I stayed to listen, then decided to ask more questions. After hearing all the amazing things about the City of Disciples, I decided that's exactly what I needed. I went back to the hospital to get my car. I sold my car, my house and everything inside and came here to get closer to God."

The leader offered the disciple an embrace. "I'm so glad you chose to join us and would like to stay here. You are free to go back to your room. Head up the stairs and into my office. Martin and Skylar are up there waiting."

Ray slid off the bed down to his knees in front of the leader for a blessing. "Thank you so much,

Leader. We love being in the City of Disciples and don't want to leave."

Azril placed his hand on top of Ray's head, then assisted the disciple to his feet. Ray followed behind the leader up the stairs as they joined Martin and Skylar in the office. As soon as the leader and his disciples guard made eye contact, he motioned toward Ray and Martin nodded. Once he received the acknowledgement, Azril headed back down to isolation room four.

As he unlocked and opened the door, he saw Murphy sleeping on the bed. He wasn't reading the supplied Disciples Doctrine, nor was he praying. Azril really wanted to know why Murphy, being a level four disciple, wanted to leave the confines of the City of Disciples. . The leader cleared his throat in order to get Murphy's attention.

Once the disciple opened his eyes and sat up on the bed, Azril walked over and sat down on the bed next to him. "Alright Murphy, tell me what is going on."

Murphy rubbed the sleep out of his eyes and yawned. "Luke had approached me and told me he didn't like his job assignment. I basically told him that we were getting paid to do the easiest jobs. We have meals and housing and we don't have to worry about the stresses from the real world. He told me we should leave the City of

Disciples so we could do whatever we want, rather than being told what to do. I informed him that I wasn't sure that was a good idea, but I was open to getting the opinions of the other disciples to see what they think. That's why we were talking to the others."

Azril rubbed his forehead. "So, you are telling me that Luke is the one who wanted to leave and you were just brought into the conversation? You didn't in any way instigate the topic from the others?"

Murphy shook his head, adamantly. "I just asked them if they felt the same way as Luke. I was wondering how many other disciples were wanting to leave because they hated their work detail. Once I had an idea of how many others felt the same as Luke, I was going to bring it to the attention of my tier leader."

Azril wanted to give the disciple something to think about before he left the room. "Well Murphy, for now you will stay in isolation for the next three days in order to engage in self reflection. I will be sure to have a dinner tray delivered to you. Please read through the Disciples Doctrine and familiarize yourself with isolation and shunning. When I visit tomorrow, we will revisit the option of whether you are released back into the city, or if you stay here for the full three days with the possibility of being shunned."

Miranda and Heather gave the same account of the situation as Skylar and Ray, so Azril allowed them to go as well. He wanted to know what brought them to the City of Disciples, but felt like he really needed to deal with the outsiders. He decided to have them stop by the office before their work detail the next day instead and led them up the stairs out of the isolation area. Martin was still in the office with Skylar and Ray when the three of them arrived at the top of the stairs.

After he closed and locked the hatch to the isolation chambers, Azril approached his disciples guard, who was standing against the door that led out into the worship area. "Martin, what is taking them so long?"

Martin shrugged his shoulders. "I don't know. I haven't heard any chatter on the walkie talkies."

Azril cracked the door open and peeked out. "Stay here with the disciples and I will go find Cory and see if they are possibly having an issue."

Just as the leader closed the door to the office, Cory was heading back into the worship center. Azril stepped around to the front of the podium and waited for Cory to approach.

Azril flopped his arms, allowing his hands to fall down, slapping his thighs. "What was taking so long? There are now four disciples waiting to be escorted to their rooms."

Cory motioned toward the side door that led directly out of the worship area and straight outside. "We were taking the outsiders out behind the building. One of them tried to run away and he had to be tackled."

"That's fine." Azril walked over to the door to the office and placed his hand on the doorknob, but turned back to look at Cory. "Now go in and help Martin. One of you can take the disciples to their rooms and the other can retrieve food trays for them. All four of them will need a dinner tray delivered to their room. Also, the two still in isolation will need dinner trays delivered to them as well. It is room one and four in isolation. I don't care which one of you does what, but our disciples need to be taken care of."

Martin backed away from the door as it opened. "Are we ready to go?"

Azril stepped past everyone, as he headed around and sat down behind the desk. "Yes. Please escort the disciples to their rooms. Martin, Cory has further instructions. Miranda and Heather, I will see the two of you tomorrow."

The leader placed his elbows on his desk and he leaned his forehead on his hands, as his disciples guard ushered the disciples out of the office.

Six

Azril decided to write down a few notes about Luke and Murphy, as he waited for one of the disciples guard to arrive with the two dinner trays for the isolated disciples. When Cory entered the office, the leader stood up and walked over to unlock the hatch in the floor.

As they descended the stairs, Azril confirmed with Cory that his instructions were followed. "Did the other disciples get their food trays as well?"

Cory nodded, as he reached the bottom step. "Yes, Martin took them their trays. We agreed to split up, so the isolated disciples all ate at the same time, even though the other four were released."

"That's fine." The leader stepped up to the first isolation room with Cory close behind him.

Azril lifted the three inch by ten inch hinged flap at the bottom of the door and Cory slid the tray into the room for Luke. The leader repeated the steps for Murphy's food tray before Cory and Azril ascended the stairs and headed back up to the office.

The leader closed and locked the hatch to the isolation, as the two of them stepped up into the office. "Thank you, Cory. Could you please have the other disciples guard bring the outsiders back in, so I can deal with the potential threat. They will most likely be placed in isolation after I talk to them. I will give them the chance to either join us, or be shunned tomorrow during the worship service."

Cory headed out to the worship area, with Azril close behind. "They are out back. I'll inform the others that they can bring them back in."

The head disciples guard ran out the side door and the leader sat down at the edge of the stage.

It was only a few moments before the disciples guard brought in the four outsiders and forced them down onto their knees, facing the disciple benches, with their backs to the leader.

The leader stood up and walked back and forth behind the outsiders, making sure that their hands were secured by the zip tie cuffs. The disciples guard then lined up in front of the outsiders. Azril stepped up behind the smallest outsider and grabbed him by his hair, pulling him up onto his feet.

The leader turned him around and shouted at his face. "What did you come here for?"

"We wanted to see what was going on over here." The outsiders voice wavered and snot began to build up in his nostrils.

"Why is it any of your business what we are doing over here?" Azril wanted to know.

The outsider just stared at him without responding. He was trembling and tears were forming in his eyes. Azril wondered if the outsider was going to wet his pants.

The leader motioned for the disciples guard to force the outsiders on their feet and turn them to face him. "At any time you could have walked through the gates and spoken to one of the disciples guard. We would have welcomed you to come to one of the worship services. At this point, you have breeched the perimeter and will be placed into our isolation in order for you to reflect upon your actions. During your reflection time, I will also be coming in for personal worship services, so you will understand what it is like to be a disciple. Due to your actions, you will not be leaving the City of Disciples. You only have two choices at this point. Should you choose to join us, you will be released from isolation and issued a uniform as a disciple, but should you decide not to join us, you will be shunned from the physical land, just as God will shun you from the promised land."

Azril stepped up to each one of the outsiders and just stared at them, one by one, without speaking. He wanted to make sure they were aware of the seriousness of their crime against the disciples before they were shunned.

Pulling out the butterfly knife from his pocket and swinging it open, Azril placed the blade against the throat of the first outsider he had spoken with. It was more to scare him, but the leader also wanted to prove that he would piss his pants and he was right.

Azril stabbed the knife into the soiled outsider's thigh. When he hunched over, placed his hands on both sides of the knife protruding from his leg and screamed, the leader grabbed the back of his neck and shoved his face into the puddle of urine on the floor. "Are you kidding me? I had a feeling you would be the first to lose control of your bladder. I should have had my disciples guard place down the plastic sheeting we use for our shunning ceremonies. Now you're going to clean that up with your shirt."

Azril backed away from the soiled outsider, just as Martin returned to the worship area. Cory approached the outsider on the floor and ripped his shirt off, before tossing it on top of the wet floor. The outsider sniffed hard, as he mopped up his mess. Once he was satisfied with the clean up, the leader nodded to Cory.

The head disciples guard shoved the outsider into a seated position and pulled the knife out of his leg. He continued screaming and crying, as Danny pulled on a pair of latex gloves and used the outsider's shirt to tie a tourniquet around the wound.

Azril approached Martin. "Did the four disciples get taken care of?"

Martin nodded. "Yes, sir. I made sure each one of them received a dinner tray and asked if they had any questions or concerns about their safety. They all agreed they were happy here. Also, Heather and Miranda informed me that they will be meeting with you after they finish their breakfast shift in the morning. They wanted to confirm if that was okay since they were suppose to meet with you before their work detail, but they felt as though making sure the disciples were fed before they start their day would be okay with you."

"Oh my goodness! I didn't realize they were on meal duty tomorrow when I told them to meet me before their work detail. I'm glad they decided to wait until after breakfast." Azril agreed with their consensus. "Well, since this one can't seem to control his bodily functions, I'm done with the outsiders. Let's just take them to isolation. I'll have Beatrice come in and finish cleaning this up later."

The soiled outsider had to be pulled up onto his feet. Warren and Lawerence stood on each side of him to hold him up. Azril turned to enter the office as Tom and Joe hooked their arms with the second outsider, as well as David and Jerry joining their arms with the third outsider. Cory and Danny chose to escort the fourth outsider to isolation, due to him being the largest of the group.

Azril had a sudden thought, just as everyone had joined him inside the office. "Maybe I should issue cuts to the outsiders before they are isolated. They brought evil into the City of Disciples by sneaking in and not minding their own business."

"I can go get Doctor Kyle so their cuts can be

tended to before they get locked up," Sean offered.

"Perfect. Thank you, Sean." The disciple ran off to retrieve the disciple's doctor, as the leader leaned against the edge of the front of his desk. "Line them up."

The disciples guard forced the outsiders to line up behind the two chairs that were placed in front of the desk. Azril stood silently, looking back and forth between all four of the outsiders. The largest of the outsiders was glaring at the leader with his nostrils flared. Azril stood up in front of him. He figured the guy had to be between six foot five and six foot seven.

The leader puffed up his chest and bumped against the big guy. Unfortunately, his six foot one inch frame only allowed his chest to come into contact with the outsider's lower ribs. "Why did y'all come into the City of Disciples?"

"Fuck you," the outsider said, with spittle flying out of his mouth and landing on the leader's face.

Azril wiped the moisture from his cheekbone. "Nice language. I see you as being the first to be shunned and not converted."

When Azril turned his back, the outsider was able to break free of the zip ties that were holding his hands behind his back and lunged at the leader. The outsider wrapped his hands around

Azril's neck. Cory and Danny grabbed at the big guy's arms, but they struggled holding him back. David, Jerry, Martin and Lawerence jumped in to try and help the head disciples guard to control the outsider as the leader grabbed at the hands cutting off his airway.

Tom, Walter, Joe, Warren and Stephen forced the other three outsiders to sit on the floor before they joined in. The eleven disciples guard in the office were pounding on the outsider with their fists, doing everything they could think of to get him to let go of the leader of the disciples.

The outsider lifted Azril up off his feet and had the leader dangling in front of him. Azril was only able to get ahold of one finger on each of the outsider's hands and he was desperately trying to pull the restriction away from his trachea.

The disciples guard threw the chairs across the room as they grabbed at the large man. When Sean and Doctor Kyle had entered the office, Kyle reached into his medical bag and pulled out a syringe. It contained methohexital, a barbiturate sedative he was planning to inject into the outsider.

Doctor Kyle punctured through the epidermal layers of the outsiders bicep and injected the entirety of the syringe into his bloodstream. In less than a minute, the outsider let go of Azril and dropped to his knees, before falling forward and slamming his head on the edge of the desk as the drug took effect and he was out.

Azril had also lost consciousness. He was laying flat on his stomach, on the floor, in front of the desk. Kyle immediately checked on the leader, as the disciples guard dragged the outsider's body out of the way. Doctor Kyle had rushed over and flipped Azril over so he was laying on his back.

Kyle took the stethoscope from around his neck, stuck the ear pieces in his ears and placed the chest piece against the leader's chest. "I can hear his heart still beating, but I need to get him back to the medical building."

"We also need to get the outsiders down to isolation," David said.

Kyle pulled on the key to the isolation chambers, that was hanging around Azril's neck, breaking the chain it was attached to and handed it to Cory. Danny and Martin decided to help the doctor with the leader and Cory began directing the other disciples guard.

Cory walked over to unlock and open the hatch. "Let's go. They are going to take care of the leader and we are going to lock up the outsiders. There are two disciples already in isolation, so room number one and four are occupied."

The three conscious outsiders were walked

down into the isolation area and placed in rooms three, five and six. Once they were contained, the disciples guard headed back up into the office and dragged the large unconscious body of the last outsider down the stairs.

Stephen reached down to lift the outsider's shoulders. "His head is bleeding from where he smacked it on the desk."

Cory shrugged, as he opened the door to isolation room two. "Well, when we are sure the leader is going to be okay, we will send Doctor Kyle back over here to tend to the wound."

The disciples guard dragged the large outsider into the room and left him on the floor next to the bed. Just below his hairline, there was a two inch gash on his forehead. The wound left a blood trail that led from the office, down the stairs and across the floor to isolation room two.

Once all of the disciples guard had left the room, Cory locked the door and moved toward the stairs. "Someone clean this up, while I go inform Omegra about the incident."

Cory continued up the second staircase, as he made his way up to the leader's living quarters. He raised a fist to knock on the door, but hesitated. At that point he had a moment to process what had just happened and he was worried the City of Disciples might lose their leader. He decided to pray before he told Omegra about her connected partner.

"I bring to You my God, my worry and hope You are able to help me through this troubling time. Please wrap Your loving arms around me as well as the other disciples. Fill us with love and understanding for You and for the leader. If the leader is meant to stay here in the physical land with us, give us the strength to continue to follow You as he recovers. If the leader is meant to be released into the promised land, remind us all of the joy we have waiting for us, with You, in the promised land. I am a Disciple of God and I will appease You in worship." Cory combined several prayers together to fit the situation.

The head of tier one of the disciples guard lowered his head and knocked on the door to the leader's living quarters. He could hear Omegra yelling, "give me a minute. I'm slower moving these days," from inside, as she walked toward the door.

"Cory! What happened?" Omegra exclaimed, noticing the grief stricken look on his face.

Cory slowly took a deep breath. "There was an incident with some outsiders that had breeched the perimeter of the City of Disciples."

Omegra grabbed the collar of Cory's shirt with one hand, placing her other hand flat against her chest. "Oh my God, Cory! Tell me what happened to my connected partner!"

The head disciples guard gently grabbed her wrist. "Azril was taken to the medical building with Doctor Kyle."

"Oh my God!" Omegra screamed, as she rushed passed him and gently, but quickly descended the stairs that led into the office.

Cory followed her down. Omegra had crumbled to her hands and knees at the bottom of the stairs and was sobbing uncontrollably. He helped her to her feet, wrapped one arm around her waist and grabbed one of her hands, leading her through the office, down the aisle of the worship area and out of the residency building.

Omegra had stopped sobbing, but tears continued rolling down her face. "We need to get golf carts around here. This walk is absolutely exhausting for me. I'm too pregnant for this."

Cory rushed her as fast as she was able to move toward the medical building, but it was obvious, due to the fetus inside her body, that after only a short distance she was out of breath. "I will make sure to make note of that and bring it up with the leader for the funds to get one."

Omegra stopped to take a short break, in order to take several deep breaths before they continued. "No, we need five. I want to make sure that if one is gone, there is still another for some-one else to use. However, they should only be available to the leader and the disciples guard."

When they arrived at the medical building, they saw Martin and Danny standing outside the door. Omegra placed her hands on her knees, trying to catch her breath.

Cory patted Martin on his shoulder, as if he were tagging him. "I'm going to stay outside with Danny. Martin, go inside with Omegra to check on the leader."

Martin nodded, then assisted the leader's con-nected partner through the doors and into the medical building.

Seven

Omegra and Martin walked into the medical building and immediately found Doctor Kyle. He was standing at Azril's bedside, taking his vitals. The leader was still unconscious, but the sound of the heart monitor was comforting to his connected partner.

Omegra slowly stepped up to the other side of the bed and grabbed Azril's hand. "Doctor Kyle, please tell me he's going to be okay."

Kyle hung his stethoscope around his neck and leaned on the side rail of the bed. "He's stable, but I don't know what his brain activity looks like yet. I was going to give him a couple of days to see if he would wake up on his own, but if he doesn't, then I will take him for a brain scan."

Omegra touched Azril's neck. "What are these marks here?"

Martin placed his hands on her shoulders. "We had several outsiders break into the City of Disciples."

Omegra turned around so quickly, her pregnant belly bumped Martin, causing him to back away from her. "What does that have to do with the marks on his neck. Martin what aren't you telling me?"

"Omegra, I came in at the end of what happened, but one of the outsiders was strangling him when I walked in. I injected the outsider with a sedative in order to get him to let go of the leader," Kyle informed her.

Omegra slapped Martin across the face. "Why didn't anyone help him? I'm sorry, but there are twelve disciples guard and the twelve of you were unable to stop one outsider from injuring and possibly killing the leader of the disciples?"

Martin had tears welling up in his eyes.

"Omegra, we were all trying to pull the guy off of him. The outsider was stronger than all of us put together. The leader turned his back and the guy lunged at him, wrapping his hands around his neck. We all tried to stop the outsider. The only way he let go was after Doctor Kyle injected him with the needle. I'm sorry, Omegra. I promise we did everything we could."

The leader's connected partner stared at Martin for a few moments before she turned back around, kissed Azril's cheek, then headed out to the front of the medical building. She shoved the door open and stood facing Cory and Danny.

"What the fuck, guys? The two of you are the head of the disciples guard and neither one of you could subdue the outsider?" Omegra scolded. Cory opened his mouth to speak, but she didn't give him a chance. "Shut the fuck up. Whatever you have to say is just an excuse and not a solution. As soon as I know if my connected partner is going to survive, I will be performing the shunning for the mother fucker who did this to him."

Omegra headed back into the building. Tears were streaming down her face and the baby in her womb was actively twisting and turning inside her body. She climbed up onto the bed with Azril and sobbed uncontrollably. Martin tried to comfort her, by rubbing her back.

Doctor Kyle stood at the foot of the bed, writing notes on a piece of paper that was attached to a metal clipboard. "Martin, why don't you go back to the residency building and place all the disciples on lockdown until I know the severity of the leader's injuries."

"NO! He's here to protect me and my baby. Martin, go tell Cory and Danny to radio to another disciples guard to make that announcement. Cory and Danny are here to protect the leader, so they can't leave either. Ask Lawerence, or David to do it," Omegra argued.

Martin nodded without speaking and headed out to the front of the medical building to relay the message to the head disciples guard. When the door opened, Beatrice's screeching voice echoed through the building. Omegra knew that Cory and Danny would hold her off from entering, so she didn't let go of her connected partner.

"I need to see him!" Beatrice screamed at the disciples guard.

"You aren't suppose to be anywhere near the leader. Not only that, but how did you find out about what happened?" Cory wondered.

Beatrice fell to her knees, blubbering and throwing a fit like a spoiled teenager. "I am his companion. I offered myself to him, so I am just as important as the bitch in there is. Get out of my

57

way."

Cory took advantage of the situation and pulled zip ties out of his pocket. He quickly tied her ankles together to keep her from running inside. Martin then whispered the instructions to Danny.

"You can't do this to me!" Beatrice screamed.

Kyle poked his head out of the door in order to address the situation. "Guys, can you please deal with this? Either gag her, or get another disciples guard to take her to isolation. Omegra has requested silence and the squawking bird is disturbing everyone inside the medical building."

Beatrice rubbed her face with her hands. "Squawking bird? My companion is in there and they are keeping me from going inside."

Danny pulled the walkie talkie from his waist band and called for backup. "Lawerence and Sean, this is Danny, come back."

"This is Lawerence."

"This is Sean."

"Please come to the medical building for further instruction."

As they waited, Omegra laid with Azril on the bed, Martin had reentered the building and sat in a chair in front of the leader's bed. Cory and Danny were out front with Beatrice. They managed to get her down on her stomach and hog tied her after Kyle had brought out a wash cloth and a surgical mask to stop her screaming.

Lawerence and Sean ran up to the medical building and stopped in front of the head disciples guard. They both stood with their hands on their knees, gulping in the oxygen.

Once they were standing up straight, Cory gave them assignments. "Sean, you are going to stay here with Danny until I get back. Lawerence, you and I are going to take this disciple back to the residency building and place her in isolation. You are going to make an announcement about the outsiders and placing the entire facility on lockdown. No one is to leave their rooms for any reason."

Sean nodded and switched places with the head disciples guard. "Got it. No problem."

Lawerence reached down and hooked one of his elbows with Beatrice, rolling her up onto her knees. "Understood, let's go."

Cory stepped up to the other side of Beatrice and hooked one of his elbows with her in the same way as Lawerence. The two of them carried her back toward the residency building as she dangled between them. She tried to argue, but the sound was muffled under the gag.

Lawerence decided to make derogatory small talk about Beatrice with Cory, since they had a long walk. "I can't believe after all the times she has been placed in isolation, she still doesn't know her boundaries in the City of Disciples."

Cory smiled, knowing exactly what the other disciples guard was doing. "You're telling me. We were just telling the leader earlier this morning that the next time she ends up in isolation, he needs to cut the bitch so she knows her place. I just keep hoping that at some point someone murders her ass because she annoyed them and the leader won't have to make the decision to shun her."

Lawerence stopped and placed Beatrice down on her knees. "I need a break for a minute."

Cory nodded and lowered her down to the ground on her stomach. "We have a while anyway. The disciples have retired to their rooms for the night, so there shouldn't be anyone wandering the property anyway. Except the night guards."

"I sort of understand why the leader won't shun her. He feels guilty enough putting disciples in isolation. The problem is, the leader has only shunned outsiders, never disciples."

"The leader has a soft spot for the disciples because they chose to join him in the City of Disciples. Of course, there are two disciples in isolation right now that may end up being shunned, so maybe he will shun Beatrice at some point. You know, once he gets tired of her shenanigans."

Lawerence and Cory laughed, as they switched sides and lifted Beatrice with their opposite arms. As they entered the residency building, they headed straight into the office and placed Beatrice on the floor, face down. Cory clipped the shackles from around Beatrice's ankles, as he gave Lawerence a rundown of what message was needed to be announced to the disciples. He walked her over to the hatch, unlocked and opened it, then took Beatrice down to isolation.

The microphone down in isolation was only connected to the isolation chambers, whereas the microphone in the leader's office was connected all over the City of Disciples. A speaker system had been set up, just in case the leader needed to reach all of the disciples at once. There were speakers in each room, throughout the halls, in isolation, as well as all the way around the outside of the building.

Lawerence picked up the microphone that hung on the wall, inside the office, next to the door that led out to the worship area. "Attention Disciples of God. Earlier this evening we obtained a perimeter breach. Four outsiders climbed the wall to gain access into the City of Disciples. Please remain in your rooms and lock your doors until further notice. The outsiders have been contained and the situation is under control, but for your safety please remain in your rooms until further notice. The leader, or his connected partner, will announce when the lockdown has been lifted. For now stay where you are and don't open your doors for any reason. Thank you for your cooperation in resolving this matter. You are all appreciated. We are Disciples of God and we will appease Him in worship."

Cory reemerged from the isolation area, stepping up into the office. He closed the hatch and locked it, before the two of them walked through the worship center.

"You take the left hallway and I'll take the right, then we will meet back here," Cory instructed Lawerence, as they stood in the foyer area.

Lawerence nodded and the two of them walked up and down the hallways to be sure none of the disciples were out of their rooms. As Cory made his way back toward the foyer, he saw his connected partner standing in the doorway of their shared room.

Debora stopped him, as he approached. "Cory, what's going on?"

Cory reached up and placed one hand on her cheek. "We had four outsiders breach the perimeter of the city. The disciples guard were instructed to bring them into the office, so the leader could put them in isolation. Something happened and now the entire city is on lockdown. That's all I can tell you for now."

She turned her face and pressed her lips against the palm of Cory's hand before he pulled away. "Was anyone harmed in any way?"

Cory looked at his connected partner, raised his eyebrows at her, knowing that he couldn't reveal any more information without the leader's permission. "I'm sorry sweetheart, I can't tell you anything else. Just go back inside and wait for the announcement about the lockdown being lifted."

Debora nodded, completely aware that he couldn't reveal any other information. Cory kissed his connected partner on her forehead, then turned and headed back down the hallway to meet back up with Lawerence in the foyer.

"Did you have any issues with the disciples?" Cory asked, as he arrived at the spot where Lawerence waited.

Lawerence took a deep solemn breath. "Nope. The hallways were clear. Most of the disciples were probably sleeping before I made the announcement since it's almost midnight now."

Cory nodded, as they walked out the doors of the residency building and headed back toward the medical center. "That's true. Hopefully we didn't wake up any of the children."

"Did you check on the large outsider in isolation while you were down there?" Lawerence inquired.

Cory smirked as he thought about what he saw while he was down in the isolation area. "Well, I placed Beatrice on the bed in room ten and forced her to lay down on her stomach before cutting her hands loose. Luckily, I was able to get out of the room and had the door locked before she was able to get up and pull the gag out of her mouth.

"I thought about checking on Luke and Murphy, but I wanted to see if the outsider in room two had regained consciousness. I opened the hinged peep door and saw that he was still lying on the floor where we placed him. There is a lot of blood around his head. We might need Doctor Kyle to go in and check on him."

Lawerence let out an exasperated sigh. "Why? Just let his ass die in there. He didn't have a problem with trying to kill our leader."

Cory placed one hand on Lawerence's shoulder and turned to face him. "That just seems wrong, but I see your point. You know that the leader or Omegra are the only ones who are able to make that decision. With him being within the walls of the City of Disciples, we are obligated to provide him with medical care."

Lawerence nodded, rolled his eyes and they continued walking toward the center of the property. When they returned to the medical building, Danny, Sean and Martin were all standing outside the door. Cory patted Lawerence on his back in appreciation for his assistance.

"Were you kicked out of the room?" Cory asked Martin.

Martin nodded and shrugged. "Omegra decided that I was breathing too hard and she no longer wanted to listen to it, so she told me to come out here."

"Damn. Do you know if the baby is okay?" Cory wondered.

Martin tilted his head and curled up one corner of his mouth. "Doctor Kyle told her that he wanted to do an ultrasound, but she absolutely refused. She told him that he was not allowed to check on her until he knew the prognosis of the leader. She is also refusing to leave until the leader wakes up and instructs her to do so. Doctor Kyle told me that he would be sure that Omegra was fed and told me not to worry about her for now."

"So what do we do until the leader wakes up?" Sean asked.

Cory pointed one thumb at Martin and the other thumb at Danny. "The three of us have to stay here, but the two of you are free to go back to your rooms. Get some sleep and in the morning have all of the disciples guard meet us here by nine."

Cory, Danny and Martin set up post in front of the doors, as the other two headed back toward the residency building. The only thing they could do at that point was to get through the night and hope for a good morning.

Eight

The next morning, Omegra woke up before the sun came out. She was laying on the bed next to Azril, interlocking her fingers with his and kissing the back of his hand. He was still unconscious.

Once the sun peeked out over the horizon, the leader's connected partner rolled herself off the bed and made her way to the bathroom, before stepping outside. "Have the two of you been standing out here all night?"

Cory was leaning against the building and yawned. "Yes, ma'am. We wanted to make sure that no one entered the building."

Danny reached up and rubbed his eyes. "Has the leader woken up yet?"

Omegra looked down at her belly and hooked her arms up underneath. "I think the two of you should swap out with Lawerence and Sean in order to get some sleep. Cory, would you mind making sure that those in isolation get a breakfast tray first, please."

Cory nodded, as he pulled his walkie talkie off his belt. "Will do, Omegra."

The leader's connected partner headed back inside. Martin was slumped over, sleeping in a chair at the foot of Azril's bed. She gently touched his shoulder, in order to rouse him awake.

Martin looked up. "Good morning."

Omegra squatted as best as she could, using the arm of the chair to steady herself. "I'm really sorry for my behavior last night. I shouldn't have hit you. It's not your fault that Azril is in his current condition and I shouldn't have blamed you."

He shifted uncomfortably in the chair. "It's okay. You were upset and there are twelve of us specifically assigned to protect the leader from these types of situations. I don't think we were prepared for what happened last night."

As Omegra slowly pushed herself back up into a standing position, Lawerence entered the medical building to speak with her. "Good morning. I normally give the morning rundown to the leader. Am I to give that to you now?"

Omegra stretched in order to loosen her stiff muscles. "Let me pee first. This baby is putting all of its weight on my bladder."

Lawerence nodded his head and allowed her to relieve herself, again. Martin groaned, as he stood up from the chair and stretched. Several of his joints popped as he released the nitrogen bubbles in the synovial fluid that had formed as he slept.

"Rough night?" Lawerence asked him.

"This chair isn't exactly comfortable. I don't think it was meant for sleeping," Martin said, interlocking his fingers and raising his hands up over his head.

Omegra emerged from the bathroom. "Whoo. Okay, I'm ready. What's going on?"

"The disciples are still on lockdown. They will need to eat and those that were assigned to meal duty can't prepare the meals if they can't leave their rooms," Lawerence informed her.

Omegra rubbed her face. "Radio for Cory to instruct Tom and Walter on the announcement procedure and have one of them announce to the disciples that they are free from lockdown. Those who are assigned to meal duty are to go first in order to prepare breakfast. After that, the rest of the disciples are free to go eat as determined by their level. The disciples guard will announce each level as they are released. Everyone is to avoid the worship area for now and they should be doing their silent reflection, as well as their morning prayer in their rooms."

Lawerence pointed his finger at her. "I'll get right on that. What about the daily job assignments?"

Omegra slapped her forehead. "Right. Um... Just have them announce that everyone is to continue the same job assignments they had yesterday until further notice. On top of that, no one is to leave the City of Disciples. If anyone has been scheduled for recruiting, they can just find a spot where the other disciples may need assistance."

Lawerence nodded, then headed back outside of the medical building where Sean was posted for guard.

"Martin, where is Doctor Kyle?" she asked.

"He went into his office in the back to get some sleep a few hours ago," he responded.

"Can you go get him please? I want to ask him if he can give me any insight to Azril's prognosis,"

Omegra requested.

Martin nodded before heading off to the back of the medical building. Omegra stepped up to Azril's bedside. She watched his chest rise and fall, as he breathed. The fact that he was breathing on his own gave her hope that he would wake up soon.

As the leader of the disciples lay unresponsive in the medical center, Cory made his way down into the isolation area. He stepped up to room one. Being one of the head disciples guard, Cory wanted to represent the leader in the most respectful manner as he recovered. After he unlocked and opened the first door, Cory watched as Luke wandered around the small room, seemingly irritated with the situation he was in.

Cory stepped into the room and closed the door behind him. "Luke, can you please sit down?"

"Finally, can I leave now?" Luke said, with a grunt.

"I'm sorry Luke, but due to the situation and you trying to convince others to leave as well, who were actually happy here, you are facing the possibility of being shunned. You will no longer be leaving the City of Disciples on your own," Cory told him.

Luke continued pacing the room like a caged

animal. "What the fuck does that mean?"

Cory shook his head. "If you are going to use that kind of language, I am going to leave. You should really be reflecting on what made you choose to come live in the City of Disciples and decide if you would like to stay with us."

Luke growled. "I already told the leader yesterday. I don't want to stay. I want to go back to living my life free and on the park bench where I was before I came here."

"Read the prayer for strength. It could help change your mind. When the leader, or his connected partner comes in to see you, I hope you have changed your mind," Cory told him, before leaving the room.

"I won't change my mind!" Luke shouted, as Cory turned the key and locked the door.

Cory felt as though Luke was a lost cause and the leader would most likely shun him. He wrote 'possible shunned disciple' on the paper attached to the clipboard.

After replacing the clipboard on the hook next to the door of isolation room one, Cory stepped up to the next room. He only opened the peep door to check on the outsider who had strangled the leader. He was no longer laying on the floor, but there was blood smeared all over the room. The outsider was sitting on the edge of the bed, reading through the Disciples Doctrine.

When he noticed Cory looking in at him, the outsider threw the Disciples Doctrine, before charging at the door. He had dried blood crusted to the side of his face, as he slammed his body against the door.

Cory closed the peep door and stepped up to room three. When he opened the peep door to look in, the outsider was sleeping on the bed. He closed the peep door and moved on to room four. There was a disciple in that room, so Cory unlocked and opened the door to see Murphy kneeling on the floor next to the bed with the Disciples Doctrine open in front of him. Once he was aware of Cory's presence, he stood.

"Cory, where is the leader?" Murphy asked, as Cory closed the door behind him.

"I have been appointed to come in and check on everyone in isolation," Cory told him.

"Okay, well I appreciate this time of reflection. I understand the wrong that I have committed. I found the right path and would really like to rejoin the City of Disciples," Murphy told him.

"I am so glad to hear that. I will make sure you get a job assignment. Right now the entire facility is on lockdown, but as soon as it is lifted I will come get you so you can join the disciples that are within your level at breakfast. Thank you Murphy," Cory told him.

Murphy knelt in front of the disciples guard for a blessing. "I appreciate your confidence in me as acting leader, but I don't think I'm qualified to issue a blessing."

The disciple stood up and pressed the palms of his hands together in front of his chest. "I understand. Thank you."

Cory peeped in on the other two outsiders who were sleeping on the beds in the isolation rooms. He went ahead and checked in on Beatrice, who was balled up on the bed, before heading back up to the leader's office. Danny was talking to Tom and Walter in front of the loudspeaker microphone.

"Is there an update on the leader?" Cory asked them, as he closed and locked the hatch.

Tom looked over at Cory. "No. Omegra requested that the lockdown be lifted, so the city could continue running. I'm here to make the announcement."

"Who told you to do that?" Cory wondered.

"I'm guessing you turned your radio down while you were in isolation. Lawerence gave the order over the radio from the medical center. I'm just making sure they understand that when they make the announcement, it must be done with confidence and authority," Danny told him.

Cory walked over next to them and crossed his arms over his chest. "Why don't we make the announcement and the two of you can go out into the foyer and check off the disciples as they emerge for meal duty."

Danny yawned before responding. "I'm going to bed. They are just as equipped to make the announcement as we are." He patted Tom and Walter on the back and left the office.

"Okay, just don't hang out in here for too long," Cory said, rubbing his eyes before heading out of the office as well.

Tom looked over at Walter and shrugged, as he picked up the microphone to make the announcement. Walter headed out into the foyer to make sure all of the disciples didn't rush out at once. "Attention disciples, the lockdown has been lifted. However, you will be released by level. The first disciples that are able to go is anyone who has been assigned to meal duty. Other than that, please wait for your level to be released."

After the announcement was made, Tom replaced the microphone and headed out to the foyer with Walter. A few disciples emerged, ready for the day and prepared to cook for the entire City of Disciples.

At the medical center, Martin returned to Azril's room with Kyle to speak with Omegra. Kyle checked the leader's vital signs before addressing Omegra.

"He is stable. Have you noticed any movement, or twitching?" the doctor asked.

Omegra picked up Azril's hand and interlocked her fingers with his. As she wrapped her fingers around the back of his hand, his fingers did the same on his own. "He's been moving his fingers when prompted."

"That's a great sign. He could wake up soon," Kyle said.

"How about now, Doc," Azril said. His eyes were still closed and his voice was scratchy.

Omegra squealed with excitement. "Azril!"

Lawerence and Sean came rushing in. Tears were streaming down Omegra's face as she smiled from ear to ear.

"Is everything okay?" Sean asked.

"He's awake!" Omegra yelled.

"Okay, quiet down sweetheart," Azril said.

Omegra climbed up into the bed with him again and kissed the leader all over his face. "I'm just so happy you're okay."

"Has the entire city shut down because I'm here?" the leader asked.

"The lockdown was just lifted. We are back up and running. The disciples guard is taking care of everything," Martin told him.

Azril slowly opened his eyes and looked around at everyone standing over him. He felt like an animal at the zoo with the way they were glaring down at him. "Has anyone been down to check on the two disciples and the outsiders in isolation?"

"Yes, Cory checked on them this morning. As a matter of fact, Murphy will be released with his level when they go to breakfast," Lawerence informed him.

"And there are three disciples in isolation right now," Sean told the leader.

"Three? What happened?" Azril wanted to know.

Omegra rolled her eyes and took a deep breath. "Beatrice freaked out when she heard you were here in the medical center. She showed up here and threw a fit to be let in to see you. Don't worry though, Cory and Danny took control of the situation and she was taken to isolation."

Azril let out a deep exasperated sigh. "We need to set up the shunning ceremony to take place. The outsider who put me here is dangerous to not only the disciples, but to other outsiders. The other three outsiders may be able to be persuaded into joining us here in the City of Disciples and I'm hoping to turn Luke back to the message of the Disciples Doctrine. Alright Doc, when can I go so I can deal with all of this?"

Doctor Kyle removed the IV from Azril's arm and gently ran his fingers over the leader's neck. "Your trachea seems to still be intact. I would prefer for you to remain here for at least a week, but I know you're going to do everything you can to get out of here. So, if you can stand up without feeling dizzy you can go, but you will need to come back for a follow up everyday until I can clear you. As a matter of fact, I would prefer it if you slept here, just so I can keep an eye on you."

"I'll keep that in mind," Azril said, as he slowly sat up.

The leader pivoted, allowing his legs to hang off the side of the bed. He took a deep breath, then slowly pushed himself up into a standing position. He held onto the edge of the bed as well as his connected partner's hand, as he caught his bearings and was able to stand on his own.

Azril and his entourage left the medical building and headed back toward the main building. The leader had decided he would remain in his office for the day, until the worship service. The disciples were working their assigned duties throughout the City of Disciples. Each one greeted the leader as he walked past them.

Omegra and Martin sat down in the chairs in front of the desk, as Azril gently sat down in his seat behind the desk. His neck was throbbing and every muscle in his body felt tight. The three of them sat silently as the leader planned for a shunning ceremony. He decided to postpone the worship service for the day and pick up normal operation the following day.

Nine

Tom and Walter came in and out of the office throughout the morning, announcing each level over the loud speaker, for the disciples to get started for the day. Once all of the disciples were set for the day, Azril wanted to prepare the disciples guard for the shunning of the outsider. David and Jerry entered the office, carrying three breakfast trays each.

David smiled, as he noticed the leader sitting at the desk. "We are here for meal delivery. Cory says everyone in isolation gets a tray."

Azril stood and reached for the key around his neck. Frantically he pulled off his shirt and checked his pockets when he realized the chain was gone.

"Azril, Cory has the key," Omegra told him, as she picked up his shirt off the floor and handed it to him.

Azril sighed and pulled his shirt over his head. "We need to get Cory in here."

Martin pulled the radio from his belt and called for Cory. A groggy, muffled voice came through the walkie talkie. "I'm coming."

"Was he asleep?" Azril walked over and stood next to the hatch that led down to the isolation chambers, as he waited for Cory to arrive.

Martin nodded. "I'm sure he was. Both him and Danny were standing guard all night outside of the medical building."

"What were you doing?" Azril wanted to know.

Omegra placed one hand on Martin's shoulder and one hand on her belly. "He was at the edge of your bed, keeping the three of us safe."

Cory entered the office looking disheveled with his eyes half open. "I'm here, Leader."

"You have the key to the isolation chambers,"

Omegra reminded him.

Cory rubbed his eyes. "Damn, I was suppose to let Murphy out when his level was announced for breakfast. I hope he is still able to eat. Is one of those trays for him?"

Jerry looked over at David and shook his head. "We were told there were four outsiders and two disciples. Murphy would make seven and we only brought six food trays."

Azril placed his hands on the back of his neck and rolled his head around. "I'm going to sit back down. Take care of those in isolation. Bring Murphy up here and make sure he gets a breakfast tray."

Cory pulled the key out of his pocket and unlocked the hatch, as the leader returned to his chair behind the desk. David and Jerry headed down first, followed by Cory. Martin stood and headed toward the office door when they heard knocking. Heather and Miranda had arrived to speak with the leader.

"Omegra, Martin, could the two of you please give the disciples your seats? I asked them to meet me here this morning," the leader requested.

Martin closed the door after the disciples entered and Omegra stood to give up her seat. Miranda and Heather sat down in front of the desk, as Omegra and Martin sat down on the sofa in the corner of the room. Murphy emerged from the isolation hatch a few moments later, followed by the three disciples guard.

"Murphy, why don't you join us. I would like to hear from all of you as to why you chose to join the disciples," Azril said.

Cory brought the isolation key over and set it down on Azril's desk after he locked the hatch. David and Jerry left to patrol the city. Cory decided to take post at the office door. Murphy stood between the two chairs that were occupied by the other disciples.

Heather chose to go first. She took a deep breath and leaned forward. Placing her hands on her knees, she looked forlorn. "I'm only sixteen. My parents were never married, but my mother has always had a problem with being alone. Men have come in and out of the house since I was a baby. I don't know who my real dad is and I don't think my mother even knows. When I was twelve the man my mother was dating at the time started sneaking into my room daily.

"He did things to me that no man should do to a little girl. When I told my mother what he was doing to me, she told me I shouldn't be working for free. After that, she had men come into the house to violate me and they paid her. She would inject me with some kind of drug to make sure I didn't fight them. When I was fifteen, I ran away from home and spent several days detoxing from whatever she had been giving me.

"When I was stumbling around, trying to find food, I heard the disciples talking to a group of people and I decided I needed a family. I'm not ready to be alone. I have been here for about six months and I have never felt this safe before."

Omegra stood and stepped up behind Heather. She placed her hands on the disciple's shoulders. "If you are only sixteen, you should not be in the disciples housing. You should be upstairs with the leader and me."

"Heather, have you told anyone else how old you are?" Azril asked her.

Heather wiped the tears from her face with the palms of her hands. "No. I just want to be taken seriously and prove that I belong here."

"Then I am going to let you make the decision. Do you want to stay alone in your assigned room, or would you like to move upstairs until you are twenty one?" Azril inquired.

"She is in a room with me," Miranda informed him. "I had a feeling she wasn't old enough to be on her own when she was recruited, so I took her into my room and have, in a way, been mentoring her."

Omegra crouched down next to the chair

Heather was sitting in. "Thank you, disciple. Heather, if you're okay staying with Miranda, then you are welcome to continue living in the disciple housing."

Heather nodded, then reached over and grabbed Miranda's hand. "She has taken me on like I'm her child. I have never felt so much love from someone before."

Azril turned toward Miranda, as Omegra pulled herself up and walked back over to the sofa. "Tell me your story. You are on level two and from my understanding, you haven't left the City of Disciples for a few months."

Miranda sat back in her chair and reached over, placing her right hand on Heather's shoulder. "I was lost before I came here. I didn't know where my life was going. I had been separated from my husband and we were heading for divorce. We had been married for ten years and had three children together, one girl and two boys. Shortly after our daughter was born, he became controlling and wouldn't allow me to leave the house. His parents were helping him keep me contained inside the house.

"His mother would bring us groceries to the house and everyday she would stop by to criticize everything I did. I contacted my parents to help me get out, but they told me that I was married to him and I needed to work it out. One day I convinced my mother-in-law to allow me to take the children to the park alone and I just never went back. I had a friend who was willing to help me out and I was staying with her.

"Before the divorce was finalized, I had been granted sole custody of the children and managed to get supervised visits with their father. During one of his visits, he somehow convinced the social worker to leave the house and he locked her out. While she was trying to get back into his house, she smelled smoke and could hear the children screaming.

"The social worker called for police assistance and that's when she noticed the house was on fire. Before the fire department arrived, she heard four gunshots and the entire house was engulfed in flames. I lost everyone important to me that day."

"Oh Miranda, I had no idea," Heather said, reaching over and wrapping her arms around the other disciple.

Azril reached forward and patted the desk with his hands. "I appreciate both of you sharing your story with me. Heather, I'm so glad that you have gone through God's cleanse and were able to get a dark blue uniform, but you are aware that you can't go out to recruit new disciples until after your twenty first year."

Heather nodded, as she pulled away from Miranda's embrace. "Yes, sir. I have read that in the Disciples Doctrine. I am also aware that I should be in a yellow uniform. Miranda is keeping me here. She has explained to our group leader that I do not feel safe leaving the confines of the City of Disciples each time we were scheduled. He has allowed both of us to remain in the City of Disciples as long as we work on the property. We were lucky enough to be assigned to meal duty this week, so we already have a job assignment."

Azril took a deep breath, trying to decide what to do with the young disciple. "Omegra, can you please place both Miranda and Heather on permanent meal duty for the rest of the year? Just to keep them here. Miranda, I'm allowing you to be in charge of Heather and her actions as the message states in the Disciples Doctrine about children before their twenty first year."

"I understand, leader," Miranda confirmed.

Azril leaned back in his chair, flicking his fingers from both hands, as to signify the two feminine disciples were dismissed. "Okay, I would like to speak with Murphy now. Miranda and Heather, the two of you are free to go. I would like to request though, Miranda, if you could please put together a breakfast tray for Murphy so he can eat."

The two stood and exited the office, as Murphy sat down in one of the chairs in front of the desk. "Thank you, Leader. When I heard the announcement for level four and Cory didn't come down to get me, I thought I was going to be shunned with Luke."

"I'm sorry. We had a slight complication last night and unfortunately both Cory and Danny had been up all night. Cory had the key to isolation when he went to bed and there was a slight miscommunication between the disciples guards," Azril explained.

"I can see the complication around your neck," Murphy stated, pointing at his own neck.

The leader linked his fingers together on the back of his neck, as he rested his head against the chair. "So, tell me what brought you here?"

Murphy swallowed hard, remembering the pain of his childhood that brought him to the City of Disciples. "My mother died when I was three and my father blamed me for her death and started drinking heavily. I was verbally, emotionally and physically abused for my entire life.

"As soon as I was old enough to get a job, I quit school and went to work. I tried to stay away from home as much as possible. Every time I had saved up enough money to leave home and be out on my own, my father would take it from me. He told me I was never going to leave his house because I had to fix the mess I made."

Omegra stood from the sofa and walked over to sit down in the chair next to Murphy. "Do you know how your mother died?"

"I was always told that someone broke into our house while my father was at work. The man murdered my mother and ransacked the house. I was asleep in my room and the man never went in there. My father said I was suppose to protect my mother while he was away and I couldn't even do that right," Murphy admitted.

Omegra scoffed. "You were three. What was he expecting you to do?"

Murphy lowered his head, shaking it back and forth. He didn't know how to respond. "Can I go?"

Azril leaned forward and placed his hands down on the desk. "Yes. Head over to the noshery and see if Miranda has a breakfast tray prepared for you. Also, please feel free to take the morning off from your work detail. You can pick up your shift after lunch."

Murphy stood and exited the office. Cory started following the disciple out, but he heard the leader clear his throat.

Azril had a single request from his head disciples guard. "Cory, please come over here and sit down. I would like to shun the outsider tonight."

Omegra was puzzled. "I thought you were going to take the day off from the worship service and resume the regular schedule tomorrow?"

Martin nodded his head. "I agree. You should wait another day and give yourself more time to recover."

Azril leaned back in his chair. He didn't want to allow the outsider one more day on the physical land. "The outsider is a danger to everyone around him. I don't want to subject the disciples to a possible violent outburst in a worship service. Martin, how about you go ask Doctor Kyle for a neck brace for me. I will wear it today and after the shunning tonight, I will immediately head over to the medical center for my overnight stay. Is everyone okay with that?"

Martin didn't say another word. He just left the office and headed out to the medical center to request the neck brace for the leader.

Once the door to the office had latched shut, Azril continued. "Okay, Omegra. I understand where you are coming from. I also believe that you should be involved in his shunning as well, but you are not in any shape to assist in the shunning process."

Omegra slammed her hands on the desk. "I don't care. He needs to be shunned and the disciples need to feel safe. If their leader can't be safe in the City of Disciples, how are they suppose to feel safe?"

"I get it," Azril told his connected partner, before turning to Cory. "All twelve of the disciples guard will need to be ready. This guy will have to be subdued and possibly hog tied. I need you to take one disciple with you and pick up some things in order to keep the outsider contained. I do not want another incident like the one we had last night."

Cory nodded, then retrieved his walkie talkie from his waistband. "Attention all disciples guard. The leader will require each one of you for assistance tonight after dinner meal service has concluded. Please be available."

It wasn't long before Martin, followed by Doctor Kyle, entered the office.

"Martin told me you wanted a neck brace," the doctor said, walking up behind the leader with the brace in hand. "I think we need to take an x-ray of your neck and make sure this guy didn't cause any damage to your spine."

Azril leaned forward, in order to fasten the brace around his neck. "I will come in after the shunning tonight for that x-ray, while I'm there for you to monitor me overnight. Omegra has decided it would be a great time to go ahead and shun the outsider who attacked me. Are you able to bring some of that stuff for sedation, in case we need it?"

Omegra shook her head. "Don't make this sound like it's my idea."

Doctor Kyle rolled his eyes and nodded. "Trust me, Omegra. I know this was not in any way your idea. The leader believes he is the only one who can protect the disciples, when in actuality there are twelve disciples with whom he entrusted to have been loyal enough to become the disciples guard. Don't worry, leader. I will bring my medical bag with a couple of syringes. However, I suggest you find a better way to contain that man, otherwise he could potentially harm your connected partner."

"I have already instructed Cory to go pick up a few things to make sure this guy doesn't get loose this time," Azril told him.

"And you are only going to focus on the one outsider, right?" Kyle asked.

"Yes, only one tonight. I still want to talk to the other three to see if I might be able to convert them," the leader admitted.

Omegra wagged her finger at her connected partner. "What does the Disciples Doctrine say about the outsiders who come into the City of Disciples with malicious intent?"

Azril opened the copy of the Disciples Doctrine he kept on his desk and opened it to the 'Isolation and Shunning' chapter. "For any outsiders who are inside the City of Disciples that end up in isolation, they are required to participate in personal worship sessions with the leader of the disciples. The leader will determine as to whether or not the one in isolation has become a loyal follower of God as portrayed in the Disciples Doctrine and they are able to be released."

Omegra smacked her hand down on her thigh. "Come on. I am sure there is a message in there somewhere that says, 'if an outsider enters the City of Disciples with malicious intent, they must be shunned from the physical land, just as God will shun them from the promised land'."

Azril rested his elbow on the desk and held his copy of the Disciples Doctrine up. "This is the message I am going with for the other three outsiders. As for the big guy, I'm taking from the message, 'Anyone inside the City of Disciples who commits any of the evil acts mentioned in the Disciples Doctrine, will be placed in isolation for a set period of time determined upon the action. Once their time has been completed, the isolated disciple, or outsider must receive one cut from each disciple affected by their actions. As for the outsider who releases another from the physical land, after they receive their cuts, the leader must then shun them from the physical land, just as God will shun them from the promised land'."

"You weren't released from the physical land though," Omegra burst out.

Azril angrily slammed his hand down on the desk. "Do you want him to be released out into the world to potentially come back and finish the job, or can he be shunned?"

The tone in Omegra's voice was just above a whisper, as tears welled up in her eyes. "I want them all to be shunned."

The leader rested his elbow on the arm of his chair, placing his chin on his thumb and his first finger on his cheek, curling the rest of his fingers down. "Let me take care of the one outsider tonight. I will deal with the other three outsiders later, as they have been placed on the list to have personal worship sessions along with Beatrice. She is a whole other issue I have to deal with."

Omegra crossed her arms over her chest and allowed the tears to roll down her cheeks. "Fine."

"Martin, could you please take my connected partner out to the noshery. I'm sure she hasn't had anything to eat this morning, seeing as I haven't had time to eat yet today either," Azril instructed.

Martin assisted Omegra into a standing position and guided her toward the office door. "Would you like me to bring something back for you, sir?"

"Just some toast and a bowl of oatmeal. Thank you, Martin," Azril said.

As soon as Omegra and Martin were gone, Cory spoke up. "I saw the other three guys. One of them wet his pants and another one looked as though he was about to. If you want to try and convert them, I support you."

"Okay, go get the items I have requested. I'm going to go down to speak with Beatrice," Azril said, standing.

"Do you want me to come with you, Leader?" Kyle asked, as Cory left the office.

The leader walked over, unlocked and opened the hatch to the isolation area. "No, I'll be okay. You can escort me back to the medical center tonight after the shunning."

Azril watched as Kyle left the office, before he descended the staircase. Hesitantly, he walked past room one and two, heading for room ten. He opened the peep door and looked in at Beatrice. She was sitting on the bed with her legs crossed, reading the Disciples Doctrine.

"Azril!" Beatrice yelled, when she noticed him in the window. She stood and ran up to the door.

Instead of opening the door, he just closed the

peep window and headed back up to his office. His body was still sore and he didn't know if she would grab on him, or do something that would cause him pain. For the time being, he decided instead to focus on the shunning.

Ten

Azril reached into his supply closet and pulled out a roll of plastic sheeting. He carried it out into the worship area and placed the full roll down onto the floor in front of the stage. He wondered if tying the outsider to a chair that was then placed onto the plastic would help contain him. Walter and Tom entered the worship area as Azril began rolling out the plastic on the floor.

"Tom, grab that chair over there and place it on top of this plastic," Azril requested, cutting the roll.

Walter walked over to assist the leader with the roll. "I hear we're shunning the big guy. How about we open this up and lay a second layer down, just in case he bleeds a lot. We could also drape more plastic sheeting over the chair to ensure easy clean up."

Azril pointed the scissors, he was holding in his hand, at Walter. "Good thinking."

Once the shunning area had been staged, Cory arrived with several bags of supplies. He set the bags down on the first disciple bench and began pulling everything out. "I got rope, chains and commercial grade electrical zip ties. This guy isn't going anywhere."

"Where's Danny?" Azril asked.

"He's coming. Martin stopped him to get your toast and oatmeal. Omegra was held up in the noshery with a couple of disciples and he didn't feel comfortable leaving her alone," Cory told him.

When Danny arrived, he approached the leader. "Would you like me to place this on your desk?"

"Yeah. I'll get it later." Azril waved his hand dismissively.

Danny sighed and stepped into the office.

Cory was holding the rope in one hand and the chain in the other. "Which one do you think would be able to contain him the best?"

"For now, just leave the items in the bags and bring it all into my office." Azril finished cutting the last bit of plastic sheeting, then turned to head into his office.

Cory packed the bindings back into the shopping bags, picked them up off the bench and followed Azril into the office. He placed the bags down between the chairs, as the leader walked over to his desk, picked up a slice of toast and took a bite, before placing it back down on the tray.

The leader unlocked and opened the hatch to the isolation area. Tom, Walter and Danny descended the stairs. Cory pressed his right hand against Azril's chest to stop him from following.

Azril waved his arm and pushed Cory's hand away. "What are you doing?"

"You said you were going to wait until tonight. The rest of the disciples guard won't be here until after the dinner shift and Doctor Kyle won't be available to assist until then," Cory told him.

"I don't care. I want to do this now. My entire body feels tired and I have to take care of this before I lay down," the leader confessed.

Danny popped his head up from the opening

in the floor. "What's going on?"

Azril glared at the disciples guard standing in front of him. "Cory doesn't think it's a good idea for me to do this right now. We had a plan to do this later in the evening, so no one else that was asked to be here is available until then."

Danny grunted. "You could at least look in at the outsider right now and if we have to wait until later, then we can wait."

"Are you okay with that, Cory?" Azril asked.

Cory nodded and sighed. Danny stepped back down the steps, followed by Azril and Cory into the isolation area.

The leader stepped up to isolation room two. He opened the peep window first, just to look in. The outsider had spread the blood from his head wound all over the room, along with the food from his morning tray.

"Do you think the four of you can handle this, or should I get the rest of the disciples guard to come help?" Azril asked.

Danny peeked in to look at what the outsider was doing. "Cory and I could use the chains. Tom and Walter, y'all can use the rope and Leader, you can be ready with the zip ties. As soon as you open the door, Cory and I can run in and wrap the chains around his arms. Once his arms are pinned down to his torso, that's when Tom and Walter come in to wrap the rope around his ankles. As soon as his limbs are taken care of, that's when you come in with the zip ties and attach the rope to the chains. That way, we can get him hog tied and carry him up the stairs to put him in the chair for the shunning."

Cory shook his head. "I don't think the leader is strong enough to pull this off. We really should wait until the other disciples guard are available for assistance."

The leader pushed air through his lips. "Fine, Cory. You win. Make an announcement. The worship service is going to be now, with the shunning. Get all the disciples into the worship area."

Cory hesitantly made his way up into the office to make the announcement. "Attention City of Disciples. Our leader has decided to have an early worship service today. Please make your way into the worship center immediately."

The disciples guard, minus Martin, were the first to arrive and Cory directed them down into the isolation area. Azril told them what the plan was and they all nodded in agreement. Cory brought the bags of bindings down from the office and passed out the items as they were assigned. However, the zip ties were then assigned to Lawerence and Sean.

Azril unlocked the door and allowed Cory and

Danny to charge into the room. They were lucky that the outsider was asleep on the bed. Cory and Danny were able to catch him off guard, as they grabbed the outsider's arm and forced him to sit up. The head disciples guard worked quickly with the chain and they pulled it tight, as the other two disciples guard swarmed in and tied the outsider's ankles together with the rope.

"What the fuck is going on? Shit man, I was sleeping," the outsider said, struggling to break free from the bindings.

Lawerence and Sean stepped into the room, as the other disciples guard pulled the outsider down off the bed and onto the floor on his stomach. "Get the fuck off me." They struggled to gain control of the outsider in order to thread the zip ties. The room wasn't big enough for anyone else to get into the room, so Danny pressed his knee into the back of the outsider's neck, trying to subdue him. Tom and Walter were being thrown around as he kicked his legs; bending his knees, then straightening them quickly.

Sean grabbed the outsiders ankles and pressed all of his body weight against the outsider's shins, while Tom and Walter pulled on the rope. That seemed to hold him down long enough for Lawerence to thread the zip ties through the chains and the rope.

As the six disciples guard pulled the hog tied outsider out of the room, Azril explained what they were doing. "Today is the day you are to be shunned. The other outsiders you came here with have seen the error of their ways and they are getting the chance to go out into the City of Disciples. You on the other hand, have a complete lack of respect. Not only for others, but also for yourself."

Lawerence had used ten zip ties to make sure the outsider was unable to break free. The eleven disciples guard in the isolation area picked up the outsider and followed Azril back up the stairs to the office.

"I'm going to fucking kill you all." The outsider struggled to break free, as the leader locked the hatch and the disciples guard dropped him on the floor in the center of the room on his stomach.

Azril walked up to the outsider. First he kicked him in the face to get him to stop using profane language, then kicked him in the ribs.

The leader stared down at the outsider as he coughed, trying to catch his breath, blood spitting from his mouth. "Cory, peek out into the worship area and make sure everyone is out there."

Azril walked around his desk and sat behind it to eat his breakfast. It was cold, and the toast was soggy, but he smiled as he shoveled the food into his mouth. Cory poked his head out through the door and looked around the worship area. He turned, looked at the leader and showed him a thumbs up.

Azril finished eating, wiped his mouth with the back of his hand and headed out to stand at the podium, as the last few disciples filed in. His entire body was still sore and his neck was throbbing. He wanted to get this taken care of, so he could go back to the medical center to meet with Doctor Kyle.

The eleven disciples guard lifted the outsider and emerged from the office, using aggressive force in order to keep ahold of the outsider and get him to sit in the chair. "Fuck all of you!"

They placed him down on his knees in front of the chair, so Danny could removed the zip ties. Once his arms and legs were no longer attached, the chains loosened. There were four disciples guard holding each of the outsider's arms down, that Cory secured to the chair with duct tape.

They tied the rope, that had been tied with a square knot around the outsider's ankles, to the legs of the chair. Cory then pressed duct tape over the outsider's mouth to keep him from interrupting the ceremony. Azril pulled out his butterfly knife and swung it open.

The disciples settled into their seats, as the

leader began the shunning. "This outsider, along with three others, breeched the wall of the City of Disciples last night. They were going to be placed in isolation for reflection. That's when this outsider broke free of his bindings and wrapped his hands around my throat. I spent the night in the medical center and need to go back for more testing, but first he is going to be bled out before his shunning. One cut of the knife for each disregard for the City of Disciples he displayed."

Azril stepped out from behind the podium to stand in front of the outsider. Both Doctor Kyle and Omegra stepped up next to the leader. Doctor Kyle was prepared with a syringe full of the same barbiturate sedative, just in case the outsider was able to break free. Omegra was there to participate.

The leader passed the knife to his connected partner for her to go first, then turned around to face the disciples. "We are gathered here to witness the shunning of this outsider from the physical land, just as God will shun him from the promised land. He is guilty of the evil acts of placing his hands on a disciple with the intent to inflict harm, as well as using ones own hands to release a disciple from the physical land.

"For each offense he has committed against the disciples, he will be bled of his wrong doings before being released from the physical land. If the shunned outsider has wronged any cleansed disciple, please step forward. If you wish, you may assist in the shunning."

Azril turned toward Omegra, as the entire line-up of the disciples guard got in line to cut the out-sider. None of them spoke to the outsider, they just went one by one, cutting him as deep as they could, without hitting any main arteries. The out-sider grunted under the duct tape each time the blade sliced through his skin. Thirteen cuts were issued before Sean handed the knife back to Azril and returned to his seat.

"This outsider is now to be shunned." The leader jammed the knife into the outsider's ab-domen repeatedly. The knife and his hand were soaked in blood, which caused the blade to slip out of his hand and fall to the floor, just as the outsider managed to get one of his arms free.

He swung his large arm and his forearm made contact with the side of Azril's head. The leader fell to the ground stunned, as the disciples guard swarmed the outsider once he was able to re-move the tape from his mouth. Cory picked the knife up off the floor, made his way around the back of the outsider and stabbed the blade into the outsider's neck, right behind his trachea. The outsider stopped struggling and coughed. Blood shot out of his mouth, as Cory twisted the blade ninety degrees and pushed it straight out through the front of his neck.

Cory held his bloody hands in a 'V' above his head and completed the ceremony. "God of wisdom and leader of the promised land, we bring before You the shunning of an outsider who has gone against the City of Disciples and against You. Just as we have shunned him from the physical land, You will shun him from the promised land. Be with all disciples as we forget about the shunned outsider and continue to look toward You. We are Disciples of God and we will appease You in worship."

Doctor Kyle and Omegra were on the floor next to Azril. They helped him stand and he retrieved the knife from Cory. The leader sliced open the outsider's femoral artery, before he turned and headed out of the worship center. He could hear thumping inside his head, as he walked straight out of the residency building.

The doctor and his connected partner led him to the medical building. Martin had to run through the property to catch up with them, so he could stay close by to Omegra.

"Leader, were you cut?" Kyle asked, as they entered the building. The doctor grabbed Azril's bloody hands and taking the knife from him. "Let's get your hands cleaned up, so we can see if any of this blood is yours."

Azril had a blank stare on his face as he walked up to the sink and placed his hands under the faucet. "I'm sure some of it might be mine. I think I felt the knife slip in my hand."

Kyle stepped up next to the leader at the sink and realized that he was staring at his bloody hands, but he hadn't turned the water on. The doctor turned on the faucet and assisted Azril with cleaning all the blood off his hands.

Kyle had to move Azril's hands around to rinse them off. "I see at least four cuts on the palm of your hand and I think at least two of them are going to need to be stitched up."

"Oh my goodness, Azril," Omegra said, as she grabbed a towel to wrap around his hand.

Azril shrugged. He shuffled over to the bed that he was in the night before and laid down. Before Kyle could get the stitching supplies set up and get back to the leader, Azril had lost consciousness.

Omegra stepped up to the opposite side of the bed from Kyle and smoothed back Azril's hair. "Is he okay? Why did he pass out?"

"I'm going to sew up the cuts in his hand, then I will conduct a few tests to make sure that he's okay. He could have just overexerted himself during the shunning. Let me do my job and I will let you know what I find," Kyle told her, as he began suturing the leader's palm.

Eleven

Cory and Danny looked out at the disciples in the worship area. After they had watched the leader get led down the center aisle in a catatonic state, the disciples seemed rattled. Blood was spilling out of the outsider all over the plastic. Once the outsider choked out his last breath, Cory nodded at Danny as he decided to take over for the leader.

Cory continued the rest of the worship service, as the restlessness and confusion of the disciples turned to fear and uncertainty. "Attention Disciples of God, if anyone who has witnessed the shunning needs any personal guidance, please don't hesitate to approach your mentor, group leader, or any one of the head disciples guard. We are all here to help you get through life on the physical land, as well as here in the City of Disciples."

The disciples guard's connected partners stood and began wandering through the worship area, approaching any disciples who appeared to be horrified. The remaining eleven disciples guard pushed the chair, the outsider was strapped in, over on its side.

David cut the tape from the outsider's wrists. "Do we even know this guy's name?"

"Who cares? This guy committed an evil act trying to release the leader from the physical land," Sean responded, as he cut the rope from around the outsider's ankles.

"Come on guys. We need to get this cleaned up and dump him into the shunning pit," Lawerence told them.

The disciples who were on meal duty were the first to exit the worship center to start preparing lunch for the City of Disciples. Thousands of other disciples headed out to their work duties after speaking with the disciples guard's connected partners. Several hundred disciples stayed behind and sat in the benches in the first few rows. Cory and Danny approached them, as the other nine disciples guard wrapped the outsider in the bloody plastic and dragged him out the side door in order to dismember the body.

"Tell me what is bothering you," Cory requested from the disciples.

Several disciples looked around before one of them spoke. "I'm Tara. I came here trying to get out of the spotlight. My parents threw me into show business when I was a child. I have been acting since I was six months old and forced to work in order to support my family. My entire life was spent on movie sets. I never saw any of the money I made from the work I did. The paparazzi followed me around everywhere I went. I'm twenty eight years old and have never had any privacy until I came here. My mother would force me to keep my windows uncovered in my room, so the paparazzi could get the best photos and videos of me. At least here, I'm covered and no longer being followed. Don't you think that if the leader continues to shun the outsiders who sneak into the city it will attract the attention of the police and the media?"

"We have taken that into account. The police need a warrant to enter the city and they can't get a warrant without probable cause," Cory informed her.

Another disciple stood up, stomping his foot on the floor as he rose. "I was arrested for a crime I didn't commit. The police said I match some description a witness gave, as if that couldn't match hundreds of people. When I was let out on bond, I came here to escape prosecution. We can't have the police poking around. I'm sure there is a warrant for my arrest."

"What is your name?" Danny asked.

"Why? So you can turn me in and receive the reward money?" the fugitive disciple said.

"You are a Disciple of God. Within the City of Disciples you are safe," Cory informed him.

"My name is Christian. I was just walking past where the crime had occurred and I matched a generic description. The police told me that the perpetrator always revisits the scene of the crime. I didn't even know anything had happened in that area. I lost my job, my girlfriend and my home. I needed somewhere to go to figure out what I was going to do. I have never felt more safe than I do here, except for right now," he explained.

Tara stood up. "I feel the same way. I felt safe and now with this shunning, I no longer feel safe."

"Tell me what makes you feel unsafe due to the shunning?" Danny asked.

Tara wiped the tears from her face. "The leader is the one who has kept us safe, but if he is released into the promised land who will take care of us? It will surely cause a mutiny among the disciples and we will have to escape the City of Disciples. I don't have anywhere to go."

Christian placed his hand on her shoulder. "I spent a month in jail in fear that I would, at the least, get beat to death. That doesn't even compare to the fear I feel right now. I have interacted with a disciple who seems like she could wreak havoc upon everyone in the City of Disciples if the leader were to die."

Another disciple stood to give her input. "I'm Michelle. I went out with friends to a bar and at some point I was drugged. I staggered out of the bar and fell in front of a police officer who thought I was intoxicated. I was arrested and taken to the police station. They called my mother, but she has a medical condition and she can't drive; I had her car. Around one in the morning, they told me to walk home, but I was still confused. I started walking and ended up passing out in front of the City of Disciples.

"When the gate opened, I was brought inside by several disciples. I was still confused and I couldn't remember what happened to me the night before. Through the past few months that I have been here, I have been able to remember bits and pieces of that night. Being here, I have been my happiest and felt safe. I'm still in the light blue uniform because I know that after God's cleanse I will be required to leave the confines of the City of Disciples and I'm not ready to go back out into the world of the outsiders.

"I feel like the shunning will bring unwanted attention to the City of Disciples and I don't want the police to take me again. When I was in a holding cell, the officers in there kept making inappropriate comments to me and I don't want to be put in that position again."

"Exactly! I can't go back to the life I had as an outsider," another disciple said.

"What is your name and story?" Cory requested.

"I'm Danielle. Child services barged into my parents house and took me and my seven siblings out of the home. Someone reported that my parents had too many children and they were unfit to take care of all of us. I was seventeen at the time and planning to move out as soon as I turned eighteen to make it easier on my parents.

"We were always fed and housed. We couldn't afford to eat out at restaurants, but my mother always cooked for us and my father worked two jobs to bring money home. We were all placed in separate foster homes and I kept running away, trying to get back to my parents. I was always caught before I could make it back to my parents house, but when I turned eighteen, I was kicked out of the foster home I was living in and was able to get back to my parents house, just to find out they no longer lived there.

"I wandered the streets before I came across the disciples and came to live in the City of Disciples. I have dealt with law enforcement enough in my life and I don't want them around here."

"Let's recite the prayer for strength," Cory said, as the disciples sat back down in their seats. "God, give me the strength that I need to get through this difficult time. I need strength in order to trust that the leader of the physical land is guiding me through Your message, as it is the way into the promised land. I need strength to follow Your teachings in order to make it into the promised land. Some days I feel as though I am falling away, whereas other days I feel like I am following You. Please, God, give me the strength that I need to follow Your teachings as told by the leader of the physical land. I am a Disciple of God and I will appease You in worship."

"I am a Disciple of God and I will appease You

in worship," the disciples responded in unison.

The disciples guard's connected partners gathered the disciples and ushered them out of the worship area. They were led out to the foyer area to sit and talk, in order to reassure them that they were safe. Debora, Sara, Katie, Sharon, Farrah, Samantha and Cora issued blessings to all of the disciples. They knew they weren't qualified to offer a formal blessing like the leader, but each one of the disciples seemed to relax a little as they placed their hands on top of their heads.

"These new disciples are having more trouble accepting the shunning ceremony than the original disciples," Cory told Danny, as they stood.

"They are questioning their safety and whether or not the police will barge onto the property, which will compromise their safety," Danny responded.

Cory headed toward the side door to check on the other disciples guard, turning to face Danny behind him. "Hopefully the leader will be back soon, so he can reassure them that they are safe here. He's better at calming the disciples, so they can trust that what he is doing is for the safety of the City of Disciples."

Cory and Danny headed to the back of the residency building where the disciples guard were wrapping the separate body parts in the plastic, in order to toss the pieces into the shunning pit.

Danny approached several disciples guard that were standing off to the side of the pit. "Someone has to clean up the disgusting mess this piece of shit left in isolation room two."

Lawerence swiped his forearm across his forehead. "I have a disinfectant spray, microfiber cloths, a pair of rubber gloves and container of disinfectant wipes in a bucket in my room. Samantha likes to keep things clean because of our daughter."

"Do you think that Samantha would be willing to clean the isolation room?" Cory asked.

Lawerence shrugged. "Samantha would definitely be willing, but with her being pregnant and having our daughter, she might be too exhausted. I don't want her to overextend herself."

"I understand that. She is taking care of one Godly gift and assisting in the growth of another. Allow her to rest whenever she needs it." Cory turned to face Sean. "What about if she got help, so she could rest at any time?"

Sean wiped his bloody hands on his pants. "Cora could be able to take care of that for the City of Disciples. I would like to run the request by her first before locking her into something, so she can make her own decision."

Cory nodded. "Absolutely, I understand that. I

don't want her to feel she is being forced to do anything. She definitely has the choice. I will make sure they both receive a bonus, but please ask her if she would consent to cleaning the isolation room. Thank you Sean and Lawerence."

At the medical center, Kyle had sealed the gashes in the palm of Azril's hand, taken several vials of blood and x-rayed the leader's neck. Omegra sat and picked the skin around the edges of her fingernails, while she waited with Martin to get the results of all of the tests.

Azril slowly opened his eyes and looked around. He wasn't able to move his head. "What happened? Why am I back here?"

Omegra stood and approached his bedside. "What do you mean? You walked back here after the shunning."

Kyle heard them talking and walked over to check on Azril. "Leader, you have a cervical fracture. I wanted to do x-rays before you left this morning, but you rushed out of here before I could. I was glad when Martin arrived to get you a neck brace to keep you from doing anymore damage. However, I gave him a soft neck brace. If I had known you had a cervical fracture before, I would have sedated you to keep you from leaving."

"Is that why I'm now wearing this plastic

119

brace?" Azril asked, reaching up and placing his hands on the immobility brace that was from under his jaw, down his neck and over his shoulders. "I remember preparing for the shunning and bringing the outsider up to my office, but everything after that, I don't remember."

"I wish I knew what the fracture looked like before. That way I could figure out what kind of damage was inflicted after the initial injury," Kyle said, basically scolding him.

"So what's the damage, Doc?" Azril wanted to know.

Kyle rubbed his forehead, not knowing how the leader would respond to his diagnosis. "Well, I will need an assistant. You need surgery to repair the fracture in your spine."

Omegra grabbed Azril's hand and hugged it against her chest. "Are you saying he has a broken neck?"

"Unfortunately, yes. And if I don't repair it, he could become paralyzed, or worse," Kyle responded.

"What could be worse than that?" Omegra wanted to know.

Kyle took a deep breath and looked down at the leader. "Leader, your spine is the central nervous system's connection between your brain and the movement in your body. If you sever that connection, it could go one of two ways. One, you won't be able to control any movement in your body, or two, you won't have any brain function."

"You mean this could kill him?" Omegra screeched.

Kyle leaned against the railing at the foot of the bed. "It is a possibility. That's why I placed the immobility brace on him. That way it keeps him from causing any more damage. Is there any way I can get Gayle to come in and assist me with the surgery? I know she was an ER nurse that heard the disciples speaking near by the hospital she worked at and came here after having a hard day. She would be a perfect assistant to have here in the medical center."

Martin stood up and pulled the radio off his belt. He called for one of the other disciples guard to escort Gayle to the medical center. Jerry responded and within ten minutes, the two of them were rushing into the building.

The doctor gave her a rundown of what assistance he needed. They prepared Azril for surgery and took him to the back area of the medical building to save his life.

Twelve

Cory and Danny arrived at the medical center while Azril was in surgery. Omegra was sitting in a chair in the front waiting area, hugging her baby bump, with Martin standing on one side of her and Jerry on the other.

"How is he doing?" Cory asked.

Omegra had tears streaming down her face. "He's been in surgery for almost an hour. At this point Doctor Kyle told me three different prognoses and we haven't been given an update on how it's going. What happened before the shunning?"

Danny furrowed his eyebrows. "What do you mean? We tied the outsider up and brought him up to the office."

Omegra stood and stomped her foot on the tile floor. "No, he did something that exacerbated his injury and caused more damage."

Cory looked down at his feet and scratched the back of his head. "Well, he did kick the guy when we placed him on the floor."

"So essentially, he jarred the fracture that already existed in his neck." Omegra stomped her foot on the floor, again. "Aren't the two of you suppose to protect him from injury?"

Danny rolled his eyes. "The leader does what he wants. If he wants to inflict pain on the outsider who tried to kill him, we aren't going to stop him."

"You don't even care about the City of Disciples, or the leader. Screw you Danny. Cory tell me what the disciples are doing." Omegra sat back down and rubbed her hands over her belly.

Danny grunted. "I don't understand why we are even answering to you. Technically since Cory and I are the head disciples guard, we should be taking over as leaders until he is able to resume his leader duties."

"What the hell is that suppose to mean?" Omegra sniffed hard, looking up at Danny.

Danny raised his eyebrows and pursed his lips. "I just mean that the disciples won't respect a feminine leader as much as they do a masculine one."

Cory crouched down next to the leader's connected partner. "Danny, why don't you go out and guard the doors."

Danny cleared his throat and looked down at Omegra. He squinted and flared his nostrils. "Fine. Whatever."

Cory clasped one of Omegra's hands with both of his. Placing his thumbs on the back of her hand. "I went down and checked on those in isolation. I put Lawerence in charge of making sure each one of them receives a lunch tray."

"Have you spoken to any of them?" She looked down at his hands.

"Yes." Cory sighed and tilted his head. "Luke has decided he wants to be shunned because this life isn't worth the monotony daily. He also said he's not an animal, so he shouldn't have to forage for food. I think he has been assigned to work the crops more often than he would like. As for the other three outsiders, they have all requested to speak to the leader."

Omegra looked up and made eye contact with Cory. "What about Beatrice?"

Cory placed her hand down on her belly and stood up. "She blames you for what happened to the leader."

"She blames me! I wasn't even in the room when it happened!" Omegra screamed.

Kyle and Gayle entered the room. The doctor walked up and stood next to Cory in front of Omegra, while the nurse hung back a few steps. Azril's connected partner stood and placed one hand over the other, under her chin.

Doctor Kyle reached up and placed one hand on her shoulder. "The surgery was successful. I would however like to keep him here for several days as he heals. He will be wearing the immobility brace for several weeks. I would also prefer that when he goes back to resuming normal activities, that he use a wheelchair to get around until it is safe to remove the neck brace."

Omegra wiped her face with her hands and took a deep cleansing breath. "But he's going to be okay?"

"Yes, he's going to be just fine. Have you eaten today?" Kyle asked, lowering his arm down to his side.

"I had breakfast earlier before the shunning," Omegra informed.

"Okay, well the leader will be sedated in recovery for a while. Go get some lunch and when you come back, Gayle and I will have him settled back in the same bed," he told her.

Omegra nodded. Martin wrapped one arm around her waist and offered his hand for stability. She reached up and took his hand, as they exited the medical center. Jerry followed close behind and Cory stayed back with Danny in order to guard the leader.

As they approached the noshery, Omegra turned around. "I want the key to the isolation area."

Martin furrowed his eyebrows. "Are you sure?"

She nodded. "I'm sure. I need to talk to Beatrice. It needs to be clearly stated to her that she needs to stay away from the leader."

Jerry touched her shoulder and nodded his head, before he turned and ran back to the medical building to retrieve the key from Cory. Omegra continued toward the noshery with Martin close by.

Omegra decided to get a tray of food and take it back to the leader's office. Martin retrieved a tray for himself as well. As they were walking toward the residency building Jerry ran up and handed the key to Omegra. He hunched over, placing his hands on his knees and tried to catch his breath.

"Thank you, Jerry," Omegra said, as Martin held the door open for her. "Martin, I need you to come with me when I go to speak with Beatrice. I don't trust her."

"Neither do I. I was actually going to suggest that I go with you," Martin told her, raising his eyebrows.

"I think she would probably try to kill you and steal your baby," Jerry said, as they walked into the office.

Omegra rolled her eyes at him and placed her food tray down on the desk. "Thanks, Jerry. Not only was I worried about my own safety that I requested Martin to go with me, but now I have to worry about the safety of my baby. Martin, bring some zip ties with you. Just in case."

Jerry left the office to meet up with the other disciples guard on work duty. Omegra and Martin decided to leave their lunch for later and headed down to the isolation. The leader's connected partner descended the stairs first, followed by her personal disciples guard. She stepped up to isolation room ten and opened the peep window.

As she rolled up onto her tip toes in order to look in at Beatrice, Martin prepared the zip ties for when Omegra opened the door. "She's just sitting on the bed with her legs crossed and her eyes closed."

Martin leaned over to see what Omegra was looking at. "Maybe she's meditating. I have heard her tell other disciples that she has been able to connect with God. She had said that God told her that she was to be the leader's connected partner and you are the only one hindering the true connection."

Omegra was seething with anger. She slammed the peep door closed and unlocked the isolation room door. She swung the door open and lunged at the disciple on the bed.

"You fucking bitch! I will shun you myself!"

Thirteen

Omegra was straddling Beatrice, pressing her shoulders against the wall. The disciple stared blankly at the leader's connected partner, as Martin hooked his elbows under Omegra's arms and pulled her off of the disciple.

Beatrice spoke with a stoic tone in her voice. "Calm down. This is not appropriate behavior for the leader's connected partner."

Omegra pulled away from Martin and pointed her finger at the defiant disciple. "What do you know about being the leader's connected partner? You are nothing. I will make sure that the leader gives you your cuts before you are allowed back into the general population of the City of Disciples. This is the fourth time you have been in isolation here at this City of Disciples, but I know you were in isolation a couple of times before we moved onto this property. In the Disciples Doctrine it states that any disciple who spends five times in isolation should be shunned. You should be careful, or you could be shunned from the physical land, just as God will shun you from the promised land."

Beatrice took a deep breath and raised her eyebrows. "If I tell Azril about your behavior, you could become a nothing. Don't mess with me Omegra. I can ruin your life and I will be there to pick up the pieces of the leader when he is devastated that you have to be shunned."

Omegra tried to pounce on Beatrice again, but Martin held her back. "First of all, it is disrespectful for you to refer to the leader by his first name. Secondly, you are to stay away from the leader. In no way are you to approach him, or even talk about him with other disciples. If I hear that you have been telling the other disciples that I stole your place as the leader's connected partner, I will shun you right out there during your work detail."

The disciples guard had to basically drag Omegra out of the isolation room. He swung the door closed and took the key from her to lock it.

Martin leaned against the isolation door as Omegra paced back and forth across the floor. "You need to control yourself. You can't conduct yourself so aggressively. Now let's go back upstairs, so we can eat."

The leader's connected partner punched his shoulder. "Oh fuck off, Martin. I'm pregnant and can say whatever I want."

She turned and headed up the stairs, with Martin close behind. By the time they had made it back up into the office, Omegra was bawling.

"I'm so sorry, Martin. I don't know what is wrong with me sometimes." She walked over and sat down in the chair behind the desk.

Martin closed and locked the isolation hatch, before walking over to occupy one of the chairs in front of the desk. "You're probably just hangry."

Omegra wiped her face with her hands and joined in laughter. "Probably. I should stuff my face before I speak to anyone else. These pregnancy hormones are so wild."

As Omegra began devouring her food, Martin poked at the macaroni with his fork, deciding to take the opportunity to discuss some of the disciple's concerns with her. "Well, Cory had told me that some of the new disciples were having some questions about their safety after this last shunning. He suggested that we should probably start doing the shunning ceremony down in the isolation area and hide it from the disciples instead."

Omegra swallowed the mouthful of chicken she had been chewing on to point out a contradiction. "The problem with doing that, is that it states in the Disciples Doctrine, 'a shunning ceremony must be performed during the worship service, so the other disciples may witness the consequences'. The disciples expect to witness the shunning ceremony because it is in the Disciples Doctrine."

Martin nodded. "I guess we will have to wait for the leader to recover so he can speak with them."

"Have them brought into the worship area and I will reassure them that they are safe here in the City of Disciples." Omegra took a bite of the biscuit from her tray.

"Shouldn't we wait for the *leader* to address it?" Martin told her.

Omegra swallowed, then growled at him. "So you are planning to make them wait for the leader to talk to them, when they could decide to defect by then, rather than allow me to speak to them first? I could possibly quell their concerns, so they don't want to defect."

"Shunning outsiders that sneak into the city, or come in for nefarious reasons, is God's way of protecting His disciples through the leader. That, in and of itself, should ease their worries about being here. If the leader can't protect the disciples from the outsiders, then he's not being a great leader," Martin explained.

Omegra looked at him, wide eyed. "That was a great speech. Maybe *you* should be the one to address the disciples."

Martin looked down at his food tray and picked pieces from the biscuit. "There's no way I could do that. I have no problem standing in front of the disciples with the leader, but I can't speak to them."

Omegra wiped her mouth with her hand. "How about you help me take notes and I will lead the worship service tonight. We can also take the notes to the medical center and run it by Azril before I speak to the disciples."

"Cory said the outsiders in isolation want to speak with the leader." Martin leaned back in the chair, rested his elbows on the wooden arms and held his hands out next to his shoulders. "He could try and convert them as disciples. That could show the disciples that not all of the outsiders get shunned."

Omegra patted her hand down on the desk and pushed her food tray to the side. "If you had more confidence in yourself, you would make a great leader. I should really be writing this down."

Martin crossed his hands on his stomach and looked down, smiling. "The leader has notecards in here that he is always using to write out his worship service notes. I could tell you what I would say and we can run it by the leader. I don't want to step on anyone's toes. Especially if the leader would prefer if Cory or Danny should take over the worship service while he is in recovery."

Omegra opened the top drawer of the desk and pulled out a stack of notecards and a pen. "I'm the leader's connected partner and I should be the one to take over the worship service while he is in recovery. The two of us make a great team. Now, tell me all that stuff again about how the leader is protecting the disciples."

Martin spoke and Omegra wrote down every word. He quoted the Disciples Doctrine and gave her all of the amazing messages God had relayed to Azril that were written in the Disciples Doctrine.

As they finished, Omegra straightened the cards against the desk. "Perfect, let's go to the medical center and check on the leader."

Martin picked up both of their lunch trays to drop them off at the noshery on the way. Omegra was feeling a little hopeful and had a slight bounce in her step. She felt that they could definitely soothe the disciples worries and any concerns they may have about their safety.

Fourteen

Martin and Omegra walked past Cory and Danny as they stepped through the doors of the medical center. Azril was laying awake in the room he had been in the night before. Doctor Kyle and Nurse Gayle were standing on each side of the bed, talking to him.

"Can you squeeze my hand, Azril?" Gayle cupped his hand with hers. When he lightly squeezed, she praised him. "Good job."

Omegra placed her hands on the foot of his bed. "How is he doing?"

Kyle was looking into Azril's eyes with a flash light. "He's been responding to touch and he can move his feet, hands and arms, but he hasn't spoken yet."

"That's because you never asked me a question that required me to speak." Azril's voice was scratchy and he spoke through his teeth.

"That's true. On a scale of one to ten, how is your pain level?" Kyle asked.

"I'm at about an eight. My entire body feels stiff and sore, even though only my neck was the injured part," Azril responded.

Kyle wrote a few notes down on the patient chart for the leader. "Okay, I'll be back to check on you later. I'm sure Omegra and Martin are here to give you a report about the disciples."

As the three of them were left alone, Omegra pulled out the notes she had for the evening worship service. "Martin and I want to keep the City of Disciples running as smoothly as possible while you are in here recovering. Some of the disciples are fearing for their safety. I think tonight's worship service should calm their concerns."

She handed the notes to the leader and prepared herself for his feedback. His movements were slow, as he reached out to take the note-cards from her. Danny pulled the door open and entered the medical building. He had been watching them through the window and wanted to know what Omegra gave to the leader.

Danny stepped up to the foot of the bed. "Leader, would you like me or Cory to take over the worship service?"

Azril handed the cards back to Omegra and took a deep breath, staring up at the ceiling. "No, Danny. Omegra is my connected partner and she is capable of taking care of the worship service."

"Well, we have had several disciples approach us expressing the urge to leave the City of Disciples. They want to speak with you," Danny said.

"Don't worry Azril, Martin and I will take care of the disciples." Omegra kissed him on his cheek. "Do you think the notes for the worship service tonight are enough to ease the minds of the disciples who don't feel safe?"

"I appreciate the message you have there and think it could help. The only way to tell is just to take it to the disciples. I think we also need to assure them that what happened to me is a test of loyalty from God," the leader suggested.

Martin placed his hand on Azril's shin. "We will add that to the notes and make sure that they know you are still here for them, just as God is here for them."

Omegra kissed Azril again, before her and Martin left to add more to the worship service. Danny stayed behind with the leader and Cory remained at his post, just outside the door of the medical center.

Danny sat on a chair next to the bed Azril laid in. "Are you sure they are the best disciples to lead the worship service?"

"What have *you* done to lead the disciples? At least they are taking the initiative to keep the City of Disciples thriving. Do you have a better person than the connected partner of the leader to lead the worship service?" Azril scolded him.

Danny stood up and looked down at the leader. "I'm just saying, shouldn't the head disciples guard be the ones who lead the worship service?"

Azril grunted and groaned as he tried to turn his head to make eye contact with his tier two head disciples guard. "You haven't done anything to suggest that you want to lead the disciples while I'm laying here in traction."

Danny didn't like the way the leader was dismissing his suggestion, so he decided to lecture him about his decision. "As the leader of the Disciples of God, you should be the one who leads the worship service. Even if that means that you write out what you want the person who has to take over temporarily says, they should not be telling you what they are going to say at the worship service."

Azril slowly raised his arm, pointing at the front door to the medical building. "Get out. You need to remember your place here in the City of Disciples. Please ask Cory to come in here."

Danny stomped his foot on the floor, then leaned over the leader so his face was hovering directly above Azril's nose. "If you don't take control of this situation right now, someone else might take over as leader."

He blinked a couple of times before standing upright and heading out of the building. Danny motioned for Cory to go inside, but didn't say another word.

Cory entered and sat down in the chair next to the bed. "What can I do for you, Leader?"

"I need you to put Danny in check. He could be a threat to my connected partner as well as the entirety of the City of Disciples. She is incubating the future of the disciples and I will not tolerate anyone threatening her safety," Azril told his tier one head disciples guard.

"Say no more, Leader. I will take care of it." Cory stood and headed out to speak with Danny. "What is your problem? Why did you think it was a smart idea to threaten the leader's connected partner?"

Danny leaned against the building and took a deep, frustrated breath. "I just think that the two of them bringing a message to the leader, rather than asking the leader what the message should be seems a little presumptuous, don't you?"

Cory pointed his finger in Danny's face. "That's not for you to decide. The leader appreciates their initiative to keep the City of Disciples running while he recovers. Considering the fact that you would just sit around and wait for the leader to tell you what to do, rather than actually just go out and do it, shows how much you don't really care about the disciples. You should have never threatened the leader's connected partner. That's the quickest way to get yourself thrown into isolation."

"Screw this shit. The leader is unable to fulfill his obligations and the disciples need a leader. Neither Martin, nor Omegra are the right ones to fill that position." Danny maneuvered his way around Cory and walked away toward the residency building.

Fifteen

Martin and Omegra sat in the office and re-arranged the notes for the worship service, in order to fit the message Azril added. They both looked over at the office door when they heard a ruckus happening on the other side.

Martin stood up and walked over to see what the fuss was about. He flung open the door and saw several disciples trying to get past Danny,

Jerry and David. "What is going on out here?"

Danny was holding back one of the disciples by looping his elbows with the disciple. "These disciples are insisting on speaking with the leader, but won't tell us why."

Omegra stood and walked over to stand next to Martin. "Let him go."

"Omegra, the disciples can't just storm into the office without explaining what their reason is. There is a chain of command and we are trying to control the situation," Danny defended his actions.

"Danny, let him go," Omegra repeated.

Danny released the disciple and the hubbub calmed down. The leader's connected partner pressed the palms of her hands together, touched her hands to her lips and took a deep breath.

"Danny, Jerry and David, the three of you are free to go," Omegra told them, before interlocking her fingers and lowering her hands. "I am so sorry you all have been treated this way. Disciples, please join me in the office."

Danny pushed past the disciples and stepped up closer to the leader's connected partner. "The leader asked me to get the key for isolation from you and go down to talk to Beatrice. He figured since the two of you were going to take over the worship service, I could take over the personal worship services with the isolated disciples." He reported false information.

Omegra furrowed her brow and glanced over at Martin. "Well, if the leader made the request, okay."

Hesitantly, Omegra handed Danny the key to the isolation area. Danny curled up the corners of his mouth and walked past the leader's connected partner and Martin.

As soon as the head disciples guard stepped over the threshold and into the office, Jerry and David walked down the center aisle and exited the worship area. Omegra pivoted on her heels and led the remaining disciples into the office. Martin followed behind the disciples, as the leader's connected partner turned one of the chairs in front of the desk around and encouraged the disciples to sit in front of her on the floor. The disciples guard closed the door and stood guard.

"Please, sit down and tell me what is bothering each of you," Omegra communicated to the disciples, as they sat on the floor around the leader's meditation rug, he brought with him from the original sight of the City of Disciples, that was in the middle of the room.

Once the disciples had settled, Omegra held her hands up, palms facing the promised land, for a moment of silent self-reflection. She wanted to calm down any hostility they might be feeling from their interaction with the disciples guard. "Okay, one at a time, tell me what's going on."

"I know the Disciples Doctrine tells us that if a disciple commits an evil act they must be shunned from the physical land. My question is, are we going to have to watch each time a disciple is shunned from the City of Disciples?" Ashley, from group seven, asked.

Omegra sat calmly with her hands resting on her belly, lounging in the chair. "I understand that most of you are friendly with one another, but the shunning is necessary in order to keep order within the city as well as keeping all of the disciples safe. I can see how you are having an emotional response to the shunning. Martin and I collaborated with the leader and we are hoping that the worship service tonight will ease everyone's concerns regarding the shunning ceremony."

"I guess I can wait until after the worship service before I make my decision as to whether I want to stay, or leave. What about Luke? Is he going to be shunned?" Ashley wondered.

"He has requested to be shunned. In Luke's case, he came to the City of Disciples looking for some consistency in his life. When he could no longer handle the monotony of everyday life, he tried to convince other disciples to go with him. At this point, we are honoring his wishes. However, with the leader being held in the medical center recovering from his injury, all shunning ceremonies have been placed on hold," Omegra informed her.

"We were just wondering if we could speak with Luke before he was shunned in order to change his mindset. We have all had random job assignments with him and he spoke to us about wanting to leave. Doris, Janice and I tried to explain to him that no one who voluntarily came to live in the City of Disciples would be willing to defect with him. We were trying to change his mind, but he moved on and tried talking others into defecting with him," Ashley continued.

Omegra rubbed both sides of her belly in a circular motion, as she experienced a Braxton Hicks contraction. It didn't take long to pass and she did everything she could not to raise alarm. "I will allow the three of you to go down to the isolation area to speak with Luke. If he changes his mind and decides to stay in the City of Disciples, we will allow him to start over. He will go back to the light blue uniform and go through God's cleanse again."

Justin, a disciple who had been found inebriated on the beach and picked up by the group of recruiting disciples, stood. "I was approached by several disciples who said they wanted to help me live a happier life. When I was an outsider, I was a disgusting drunk. There wasn't a single day that would go by that I didn't wake up and grab the bottle of scotch. I put it in my coffee in the morning, I mixed rum with lunch and for dinner I would dabble with vodka. I was on the road to cirrhosis of the liver.

"When the disciples brought me here I spent days, possibly weeks, shaking and vomiting all the poison out of my body. Luke was the disciple who let me stay with him until I was well enough to be on my own. He took me to see Doctor Kyle to get checked out and now I'm the healthiest and happiest I have ever been. I would like to let him know how he changed my life for the better."

Omegra reached out her hand and Justin grabbed it. "I understand. Justin, if you would like to go with Ashley, Doris and Janice down to isolation to see Luke, you are more than welcome. It would be great if the four of you could convince him to stay. I'm sure he would change his mind if he knew how loved he was here in the City of Disciples. Not just by God, but also by the other disciples."

"Why do the shunning ceremonies have to be public? Can't the leader and the disciples guard just do it quietly down in the isolation area, or something?" Robin asked, a disciple who had heard the recruiting disciples speak twice, then showed up at the City of Disciples with a large suitcase filled with money.

"That was never the plan. Basically, the shunning ceremony is performed at the worship service in order to allow any disciple, who feels as though they were wronged by the shunned disciple or outsider, to participate in the shunning," Omegra told her.

"I actually appreciate that more," Caroline, a disciple who was having a mental break and she was trying to run away from her life when she joined the Disciples of God, began. "If we get a chance to retaliate against the person who wronged us, it could keep us from committing evil acts."

"Thank you Caroline. That is the point. If the disciples assist in the shunning of a disciple or outsider, no one has any reason to feel anger within the City of Disciples and the leader shouldn't have to isolate any violent disciples," Omegra responded. "Murphy, I see you have joined us here as well. Was there anything you wanted to add?"

"No. I just happen to hear all the commotion and wanted to make sure that everything was okay," Murphy said.

Omegra stood and walked toward the isolation

hatch. "For those of you who would like to visit with Luke, I will allow you to do so in a moment. As for the others, I hope to see you at tonight's worship service. I promise the message will calm all of your concerns."

Martin opened the door that led out to the worship area and allowed some of the disciples to exit. Justin, Ashley, Janice and Doris stuck around to speak with Luke. Omegra beckoned for Martin. He walked over to her.

"Go down there and find out what Danny and Beatrice are talking about," Omegra whispered.

Martin nodded, then descended the steps into the isolation area.

Sixteen

Martin snuck up to isolation room ten. Danny had left the door cracked open just enough for Martin to listen in on their conversation.

"Beatrice, I'm telling you that this could work and it would keep you out of isolation," Danny told her.

"What about your connected partner Sara? Won't she be suspicious if we begin conspiring together?" Beatrice asked.

Danny shrugged. "I don't know and I don't care. Ever since she gave birth to our kid, I don't matter anymore. She basically used me to have a baby."

Beatrice took a deep breath. "Fine, but only if you can confirm that I will be the leader's connected partner."

With that statement, Martin headed back up the stairs into the office. Omegra was sitting with the disciples on the meditation rug. She looked over at Martin, as he climbed out from the hatch.

The disciples assisted her up onto her feet and she approached him. "What is going on down there?"

Martin shook his head. "Danny was promising Beatrice that if she followed his lead, she could become the leader's connected partner."

Omegra clenched her jaw. "I swear that bitch just won't quit. And now she's got Danny involved. Something needs to happen to her."

The disciples guard placed his hands on her shoulders as he heard someone walking toward the isolation staircase. He placed one finger up to his mouth, under his nose.

The two of them stepped away from the isolation hatch and stood next to the desk, as they waited for Danny to appear. No one said anything as he stepped up into the office.

Omegra approached him before he could close the hatch and held out her hand. "Give me the key."

Danny shifted his eyes back and fourth between her and Martin. They were both looking at him with condemnation. Danny was standing in a way that put Martin on alert, in case the tier two head disciples guard chose to flee with the key, rather than handing it over. Martin let out a calming breath, when Danny actually handed the key to Omegra. The silence was deafening as he placed the key into her hand, then left the office without saying a word.

As soon as the door closed Omegra stomped her foot on the floor and whipped her head toward Martin. "That was absolutely exasperating. I wanted to call him out, but I bit my tongue."

Martin walked over to stand next to her. "You did good. There was no reason to exacerbate the situation."

The leader's connected partner motioned for the four disciples to follow her down the stairs and into the isolation area. Neither of them had been down there, but they all had encouraging things to say to those who were isolated. Martin stayed up in the office just in case Danny returned.

Omegra unlocked and opened the door to isolation room one. "Luke, these disciples have had some very nice things to say about you and they would also like to speak with you before you make the final decision about shunning."

Luke stood and embraced Ashley, Doris and Janice. "What are y'all doing here? And Justin, are you okay? You aren't drinking again, are you?"

"No. I just don't know how I could make it through life without you. You were the first disciple to take me in and helped get me through a rough time in my life," Justin told him.

Ashley sat on the bed and touched Luke's fingers. "Please stay. I know they could find a work assignment that you're happy with. There is no reason to defect. I'm worried that if you were to even leave, something bad could happen to you among the outsiders. If you are shunned, we won't be able to see you in the promised land."

Janice leaned against the wall next to Luke. "The leader has decided to allow you to stay, as long as you agree. The only stipulation is that you are required to go back to the beginning and go through God's cleanse again, in order to reacquaint yourself with the power of the disciples."

"Okay, look. I don't really have a problem with anything going on here. What I do have a problem with is the fact that when I was an outsider, I made all my own decisions. I didn't have a schedule and I wasn't told what to do and when to do it. I just wanted to go back to being free," Luke admitted.

Doris stepped over and sat down on the bed next to Ashley. "We *are* free here. The disciples never have to worry about when their next meal is coming, or if we have enough money for groceries even to just eat. None of us are fighting over who makes more money, or who has nicer clothing. The leader, his connected partner and the disciples guard have done everything to make sure we are taken care of. When you were an outsider, nothing was guaranteed. Your meals and your safety was not guaranteed."

"Omegra, is it true that I can start over and stay here?" Luke asked, looking around at the disciples who surrounded him.

Omegra nodded. "Yes. You are a disciple and were able to level up with recruiting new disciples. Due to your attitude and disrespect, I feel as though you should reacquaint yourself with the Disciples Doctrine and God's message."

"Does that mean I can get out of here now?" Luke wondered.

The leader's connected partner thought for just a moment. She didn't want it to be that easy for him to just get out of isolation. She wanted him to prove that he knew what he did was wrong. "If you can tell me what evil act you committed that led you into isolation and how you will change."

Luke nodded. "I feel like there is more than one. First, I showed disrespect toward both God and the leader by not appreciating the City of Disciples. Second, I feel like I was treating the other disciples as if they weren't equal to me. I know that if I would have brought my concerns to either you or Stephen, the leader would have sat down with me and the whole situation could have been avoided."

Omegra placed her hand on her belly. "I'm so happy you have learned the error of your ways. Your sentence was for three days, but I'm going to release you a day early for loyal behavior."

"So I'm free to go?" Luke inquired.

"Yes. I will take you to Emma to change out your uniforms. First, would the five of you be willing to speak with the outsiders?" Omegra wanted to know.

"Absolutely! I would really enjoy converting the outsiders who snuck into the City of Disciples," Ashley said, bouncing up onto her feet.

"Omegra! Can I talk to you?" Caroline bellowed from the top of the stairs to the isolation.

The leader's connected partner opened the three isolation rooms the outsiders were occupying and left the disciples to speak with them. She headed over to the bottom of the stairs and looked up to the hatch. "Caroline, come on down."

Caroline descended the stairs. "I was just wondering if I could speak with Beatrice. She may need someone who is not connected to the leader to get her to understand how inappropriate her behavior has become. She seems to be getting worse."

"I think that would be okay. She needs to change, or the leader may be inclined to shun her," Omegra admitted.

"I will take care of it," Caroline told the leader's connected partner. "The last conversation I had with her, she seemed delusional."

Omegra walked with Caroline over to the isolation room Beatrice was locked in. She unlocked and opened the door, allowing the disciple to enter, then closed the door. The leader's connected partner did not want to enter the room, or even see Beatrice.

When she rejoined the other disciples who were with the outsiders, they were all laughing and seemed to be having a great time. "Have y'all told the outsiders about the City of Disciples?"

"Yes and they are willing to stay," Justin informed her.

"That's great. I'm so glad to know that they were able to see the way of the disciple. Let's get those of you who require a light blue uniform, over to Emma," Omegra said.

The disciples, along with the outsiders headed up into the office. Omegra went back to open the door to the isolation where Caroline was with Beatrice.

Caroline emerged alone and closed the door behind her. "She is refusing to leave until she can speak with the leader. There isn't anything anyone can say to get her out of there until she is able to speak with him."

Omegra locked the door, leaving Beatrice behind. "Fine, then she will stay in there without any contact with any disciple for at least three months. I will make sure she gets food, but that's it. No one will talk to her and she will only have the Disciples Doctrine to keep her company."

When they arrived back up into the office, Martin was talking to the others, waiting for Omegra to return. "It's good they were able to convince the outsiders to join the disciples."

"It absolutely is. They are needing to find Emma for uniforms. Could you please call Danny in, so I could speak to him about his behavior with the disciples," Omegra requested, as she locked the hatch.

Martin opened the door to the office, allowing the disciples to depart as she sat down behind the desk. The tier three head disciples guard called over the walkie talkie for the tier two head disciples guard.

Danny had to have been close by. It didn't take long for him to arrive to the office. "What can I do for you, madam leader?"

"Danny, the City of Disciples is to be a halidom for the disciples. We never want them to feel unsafe, or that the disciples guard is free to get violent with them," Omegra explained. "Why would you put your hands on a disciple who was looking for guidance?"

"It wasn't planned to restrain them, but they were insisting to barge into the office. They weren't wanting to listen to reason, nor would they wait for us to announce them," Danny defended himself.

Omegra slammed her fist down on the desk. "If the disciples want to speak with the leader, they are able to approach either the disciples guard, or even me at any point. It doesn't matter on how their approach is. The leader is in the medical center recovering and I'm the one taking over until he is able to join us again. However, I'm still only the leader's connected partner. That means that I am still within the chain of command."

Danny shrugged, as he raised his eyebrows and pursed his lips. "I wasn't being violent, or aggressive in any way. I was restraining an unruly disciple who was unwilling to listen to reason."

She leaned back in the chair and rested her hands on her belly. "If they feel as though you were being aggressive, that should be addressed. You should have allowed them to enter the office, so this wouldn't be a problem now. Were you afraid they were armed?"

He shook his head. "I never thought any of them were armed with a weapon, nor did I think they were going to cause any harm to you, or anyone else."

Omegra rubbed her face with her hands. "If they were unarmed and just wanted to talk, why would you keep them from entering the office?"

"The disciples are required to go through the chain of command, but they were refusing to allow me, as the head disciples guard, to be a part of that chain." Danny shifted his weight from his left leg to the right. "Those disciples wanted to surpass me and go directly to the leader."

"Danny, can we please work together to be sure that each disciple here within the City of Disciples feels safe." Omegra leaned forward with her forearms resting on the desk. "Also, I am technically on the same level as you are when it comes to the chain of command. That includes when it comes to who is going to lead the worship service."

Danny pursed his lips and took a deep breath. "I get it. You are the leader's connected partner and you're the one who gets to lead the worship service."

Omegra rubbed her temples with two fingers from each hand. "I guess we aren't going to get any where. You think you were right with your actions and until the leader says otherwise, you are just going to stand there and act condescendingly toward me? You can go. I'm done talking to you."

Danny turned and headed toward the office door. Before he left, he swiveled around and glared at Omegra. "Just because you're the leader's connected partner, doesn't mean that you're the one who will take over the disciples if the leader is released into the promised land."

Omegra furrowed her eyebrows, flared her nostrils and clenched her teeth. "Azril trusted you as a loyal disciple. He assigned you to head disciples guard with Cory. Unfortunately, your actions lately have caused me to question that decision. Due to the fact that you *are* part of the disciples guard, you are exempt from isolation. However, I can remove that title from you just as quickly as

Azril assigned it to you. You need to go to your disciple housing, read the Disciples Doctrine and remember your place, or you won't be a member of the disciples guard any more. If your actions continue to be aggressive toward the disciples, or even me, you will be stripped of your title and placed into isolation with the option of being shunned."

"I will just keep my mouth shut and bring it up to the leader when he gets out of recovery," Danny said, interlocking his fingers together just below his chin. "We will find out then who would be a better fit to take over to the disciples."

"Take tomorrow off and use that time to read the Disciples Doctrine and reflect upon your actions. Now go, before I take it upon myself to throw you in isolation," Omegra told him, as Martin opened the door to the office to allow Danny to exit.

Omegra prepared for the worship service as the disciples began entering the worship area to hear the message. The leader's connected partner took a deep breath, looked at Martin and nodded. The two of them headed out of the office to share the message.

Seventeen

"Disciples of the city, please find a seat quickly. I have a message from the leader," Omegra said, standing behind the podium. She waited for all of the disciples to get settled and quiet. "Thank you for joining me tonight. The leader and I understand that several of you have some concerns about the shunning ceremony. I can completely see where your concerns are coming from. However, shunning outsiders who sneak into the City of Disciples, or come in for nefarious reasons, is God's way of protecting His disciples through the leader.

"That, in and of itself, should ease your worries about being here. If the leader can't protect the disciples from the outsiders, then he's not being a great leader. The leader of the disciples was being tested by God and that is why he is now in the medical center recovering from an injury that was inflicted by an outsider who had breeched the wall surrounding the City of Disciples.

"In good news, the three other outsiders who snuck into the City of Disciples with the shunned outsider have decided to convert as a disciple. They are here with us tonight. Please make sure you all make them feel welcome here.

"While the leader is recovering, please feel free to bring all of your concerns to either me, or any one of the disciples guard. We are willing to assist you in any way possible. I would like to open the worship service for discussion, if anyone has any questions."

As several disciples stood up and made their way down the center aisle, Martin stepped up in front of the podium. "Before you ask your question, please state your name first. With there being several thousand disciples living in the City of

Disciples, you can't expect Omegra to know your name."

Martin moved back over to the side of the stage, as the first disciple stepped up. "My name is Ruth. I was an escort who approached a disciple as he was filling up the shuttle. He told me that I shouldn't have to sell myself just to live. When I learned about the disciples and how happy everyone was in the City of Disciples, I decided to take a chance.

"I had been beat on, stabbed and choked, but I needed the money in order to pay my bills and live. I couldn't believe that there was a place I could live happy and work safely without having to worry about how I would pay my bills. Now we are having to worry about the disciples guard getting violent. Is there anything you are able to do to reassure the disciples that the disciples guard won't start beating us?"

"I'm absolutely appalled that any disciple would feel that the disciples guard would be violent towards them. Since Cory is at the medical center with the leader, is there a way that any of the other disciples guard can explain this?" Omegra said, placing her fists on her hips.

David stepped forward and addressed the leader's connected partner. "I might be able to shed some light on that."

Martin noticed Omegra rubbing her back, seemingly to be in a lot of pain from standing for as long as she had. He grabbed a chair and placed it in front of the podium and assisted her to the seat.

"Thank you, Martin. This baby is putting pressure on every bone in my body. Now David, tell me what you know," Omegra said.

"Don't you dare, you little bastard," Danny called from the left side of the stage.

"Danny, is there something you would like to say?" Omegra asked.

Danny crossed his arms over his chest. "There is nothing to say. David doesn't know what he is talking about."

Omegra pointed her finger at Danny. "Lawerence and Jerry, take care of that. David, go on. Tell me what you know."

Lawerence grabbed Danny from behind, wrapping his arms around Danny's chest, pinning his arms against his body. Lawerence forced Danny out of the side door, followed by Jerry.

David stepped closer to the leader's connected partner and knelt down in front of her. "Danny says that if the leader is no longer able to fulfill his duties as the leader of the disciples, then one of the disciples guard should be the one to take over the City of Disciples. When I asked him who he thought should be the one to take over, he said he was the only disciples guard worthy to be the leader."

"Is that all he said?" Omegra asked.

"He said that he would shun anyone who got in his way from taking over," David admitted.

"Thank you, David. I appreciate your loyalty. As for the rest of the disciples guard, do any of you feel as though I'm unfit to take over while the leader is in the medical center recovering?" Omegra addressed the remaining seven disciples guard.

None of them spoke. They all knelt down in front of Omegra and accepted her as their temporary leader. Within a few seconds, all of the disciples were kneeling.

Omegra leaned over toward Martin, who was the closest to her and whispered. "I'm afraid that if Danny doesn't change his actions, as in being aggressive with the disciples or being loyal to the leader, he may be demoted from disciples guard and could possibly end up in isolation."

"If Danny ends up being shunned, who would take his place in the disciples guard?" Martin asked.

"I hope we never have to worry about that, but for now, I need you to stay with me at all times. Do you think Farrah would be willing to join you by my side until Azril can be discharged?" Omegra requested.

Martin motioned for Farrah to join him up on the stage. "She would be honored to keep you and your baby safe."

As Martin explained to Farrah what was expected of her, Omegra continued with the disciples. "Does anyone else have any concerns about anything within the City of Disciples?"

Thousands of disciples bowed their heads, in acceptance to Omegra being the temporary leader. As she looked out into the worship center, the leader's connected partner was trying to figure out what they were going to do about Danny. She felt as though she needed to speak with the leader in order to gain control of the disciples guard.

The disciples were growing so quickly. Omegra felt as though they should suspend any recruitment job assignments until the leader was able to return to his post. The City of Disciples had enough money to function for at least a decade with the disciples they currently had, so she figured three months of stagnation shouldn't cause them to go broke.

Any changes she made had to be approved by the leader first in order for the chain of command to be strong. Any kink in the chain could potentially bring down the entire city and the disciples would cease to exist. God's message for the disciples was important for them.

Omegra was assisted into a standing position by Martin and Farrah. "Disciples, I appreciate everyone's loyalty to the City of Disciples. If anyone has any issues, at all, that you would like to discuss privately, please do not hesitate to request a meeting with me. Any one of the disciples guard has the ability to radio in to Martin for the request. He will be with me at all times and I trust him. I understand for those of you who have been slighted by Danny and I assure you that he will be taken care of promptly. Please go and enjoy the rest of your evening."

The leader's connected partner raised her arms out at shoulder height, with the palms of her hands facing the disciples and bowed her head. She prayed to God for guidance as she accepted her role as the temporary leader of the disciples. "God of wisdom and leader of the promised land, please guide us as we do what we can to understand Your teachings through our leader of the physical land. Guide us to make the right decisions in the physical land, in order for us to meet You in the promised land. We need the leader of the physical land to show us the way to You in the promised land. Guide us into trusting that the leader is directing us on the correct path. Know that each day we look to the leader of the physical land to guide us to the promised land. Fill our hearts with trust that You have chosen the best leader of the physical land. We are disciples of God and we will appease You in worship."

The entire worship area responded simultaneously. "We are disciples of God and we will appease You in worship."

The disciples filed out of the worship center and Omegra gave instruction to Martin and Farrah. "We need to first go talk to Danny and make sure that he understands his place here in the City of Disciples. After that, the three of us will go see the leader and let him know what is going on."

Eighteen

They headed out the side door, approaching the three disciples guard. Lawerence and Jerry were basically scolding Danny for his actions.

"Omegra is the same as the leader. She is to be treated with the same respect," Lawerence told him.

"I work for a masculine leader. The leader is the one who deserves respect. There is a specific role that the feminine have and commanding respect from the masculine isn't that role," Danny responded, as Martin, Omegra and Farrah approached.

Jerry crossed his arms over the top of his head. "The disciples are about acceptance, equality and tolerance. Every disciple is equal and there aren't specific roles just because the disciple is either feminine or masculine. That is the entire message the leader has been giving us from God through the Disciples Doctrine."

Danny turned to face the leader's connected partner. "I can't look at you and see an equal. That includes Sara. She understands that as my connected partner she is there to support me. That is her role. The feminine in the relationship is meant to support the masculine. If the masculine can't perform the duties he is meant to, another masculine disciple should take over. Being the leader of the disciples is a masculine job, not a feminine."

"That's not how this works. Connected partners are to be supportive of each other. If one is assigned a job duty and they are unable to fulfill that job duty, the connected partner is to help with getting that job completed. This is why all of the disciples are assigned to meal duty and not just the feminine. All disciples are assigned to take care of the livestock and not just the masculine. Your mindset is that of an outsider and not a disciple," Omegra chastised.

Farrah stepped up closer to Danny. She was angry. "So Danny, where do you think Martin and I fit into your mindset? We came here just wanting to be treated with respect for being who we are. Never once have I ever felt as though that I wasn't equal to everyone else here and the leader has treated me as a person. As an outsider, I was generally treated like trash and less than human. You are thinking like an outsider and you are suppose to be the head disciples guard, just like my connected partner, Martin."

"I'm not speaking to either of you. The two of you decided you weren't happy in the bodies that God gave you at birth, so I don't see either of you as equals." Danny turned toward the other disciples guard. "Lawerence, Jerry, I'm only willing to speak with the two of you, the leader, or any of the other disciples guard. We are in need of a new leader, since the current leader is unable to fulfill his job duties, I think that either Cory or I would be a better fit to take that over."

Omegra stepped up in front of Danny, with her back to him. "Lawerence, you are in charge of taking him to Cory and allowing the tier one head disciples guard to take care of what happens. He is in danger of being demoted from disciples guard and I will put Sara in his place to take over, if he can't understand God's message as written in the Disciples Doctrine."

Lawerence grabbed Danny's arm and led him away toward the medical building, as the others waited a few moments before they, as well, headed in the same direction to visit with Azril. Farrah was fuming from Danny's response.

Farrah walked next to Omegra. "Being a disciples guard and a head disciples guard at that, you would think that he would be more of a loyal disciple."

Omegra saw Lawerence and Danny standing outside of the medical center as they approached. "The problem is, he was a loyal disciple until the leader ended up with an injury. Now Danny has turned back to his outsider, misogynistic mindset. The fact he is only willing to follow the leader of the disciples if it's a masculine leader, tells me that he is not the right fit to be a disciples guard. That means that he isn't treating all of the disciples equally."

"Do you think Sara would be able to handle the responsibilities of the disciples guard?" Martin asked.

"Absolutely. I spoke with her before she became Danny's connected partner. She is a strong, loyal disciple and I'm sure she will demand respect as a disciples guard," Omegra admitted.

"If you think Sara can handle it, you should probably prepare her for the possibility and make sure she would be willing to report anything that Danny could be doing that is harming the City of Disciples," Farrah suggested.

Azril slowly opened his eyes as Omegra approached the bed. Cory was sitting in the chair next to him. "What has Danny done now?"

"What makes you think Danny did anything wrong?" Omegra said, not wanting to worry the leader.

Azril chuckled. "My hearing works just fine and this building isn't that large. I heard y'all discussing Sara and Danny. That means that Danny has again upset the disciples and now you are trying to figure out how to fix it, along with keeping the twelve disciples guard. Also, Lawerence has already come in here and said he needed Cory to help him with an issue."

"Leader, I think that he may be reverting back to outsider mentality. He doesn't see all the disciples as being equal. As well, he believes that the job assignments are gender specific," Farrah informed him.

Azril contorted his mouth into a sinister smile. "Omegra, for tomorrow's job assignments, I want you to put Danny on laundry duty in the morning, and meal duty for dinner. As a matter of fact, put him on those job duties for a full week. If he has a problem with that, he can come speak to me. Make sure that Sara is appointed to the disciples guard during that time and have her shadow Cory."

"Thank you, Azril," Omegra said, as Cory stood up and allowed her to sit in the chair next to the bed.

"Farrah, you will also be set as a disciples guard, but only as a backup with Martin for now. I would like to get you a grey uniform to match your job duty. Since Martin is the personal disciples guard to Omegra, Farrah, I would like you to be the personal disciples guard to our baby," Azril told her.

A single tear rolled down Farrah's cheek. "I would absolutely appreciate that. I promise, I will stay with Omegra as long as she is carrying that baby. I will do everything I can to keep her safe and to protect the baby. Thank you so much, Leader."

"Have Danny give Sara his walkie talkie so she can stay in touch with all the other disciples guard," Azril said.

"What happens if Danny refuses?" Martin wondered.

"If Danny refuses, Cory you will have to bring

him to me and I will deal with it. At this point, I'm in danger of having my position as the leader being challenged. I may need to have a meeting with the other disciples guard to make sure they are still loyal to me as the leader of the disciples." Azril felt as though he could take care of Danny, so he changed the subject. "I don't have anything else to say about this situation. Tell me about the ones in isolation."

Cory left, in order to deal with Danny. He was sitting on the ground outside of the medical center with Lawerence standing over him.

Nineteen

Omegra touched the leader's hand. "Everyone has been released from isolation, except Beatrice. She is the last one left. There were several disciples who pleaded with me to speak with Luke in order to convince him to stay. When he agreed to stay in the City of Disciples, they decided to speak with the outsiders and converted them into disciples."

"That's amazing. As soon as I am able to get out of here, I would like to meet with the three new followers. Also," the tone in Azril's voice changed. "Please tell me that you didn't just leave Beatrice in isolation because you didn't want to deal with her."

"She might be that petty, but I am not. I tried speaking with her earlier in the day and she refused to talk to me. She also said that she was going to tell you that I don't conduct myself in a way that suggests that I am worthy of being your connected partner." Omegra leaned back in the chair.

Martin placed his hand on her shoulder. "You did pounce on her and tried to strangle her."

Omegra began to cry. "She knows exactly what to say to get under my skin. Beatrice has been trying to steal Azril from me since the first day we met her."

Azril took a deep breath. "You can't let her get to you. Plus, Doctor Kyle says I could be staying here for three months. You are going to have to run the City of Disciples the same way I would. That means you need to remain calm and not let Beatrices behavior affect the way you treat her."

"I know, but she is just so irritating." Omegra placed her elbows onto her knees and buried her face in her hands.

"Tell me what happened down in isolation with the outsiders." Azril carefully shifted his body, trying to get more comfortable.

"Well, while the disciples were speaking with the outsiders, another disciple was speaking with Beatrice. She told that disciple that she wasn't going to leave isolation until she could speak with the leader," Omegra said, lifting her head up.

Martin cleared his throat. "What about Danny?"

"What about Danny?" Azril repeated.

"Danny went down to speak with Beatrice after you talked to him this morning. He said that you instructed him to conduct the personal worship service with her, since Omegra was in charge of the worship service for the entire City of Disciples." Martin crossed his arms over his chest.

Azril furrowed his eyebrows. "I never told him that. That must have been right after I told him that his behavior was inappropriate, then instructed him to send Cory in so I could speak with the tier one head disciples guard. I have suspected for a while that Danny had a narcissistic personality. When I joined Danny and Sara as connected partners she was so happy. However, right after their son was born, Sara's happiness seemed to wane at times. Any time she was smiling, or laughing with the other disciples and Danny would walk by, she would immediately put her head down and become stoic. Do you know what Danny and Beatrice were talking about?"

Martin took a step forward to see the leader's face better. "I caught the tail end of the conversation, but it sounded like he was making a plan with Beatrice to help her become your connected partner."

Azril slammed his fist down next to him on the bed, then grunted as pain radiated through his body. "That sounds like a threat to Omegra."

Sharon and Caroline rushed into the medical building, arguing back and forth as to which one was going to inform the leader of the information they had. Neither of them wanted to tell him, but they knew he had a right to know.

However, Sharon had apparently lost the argument and stepped up to the foot of the bed. "Leader, we have some information regarding a disciple who is trying to cause issue with your connected partner. This disciple was trying to convince others that Omegra is ill-equipped to be your connected partner, nor should she be allowed to take over as the leader of the disciples."

"Why am I being attacked?" Omegra cried.

Azril squeezed her hand. "Which disciple is this?"

Caroline stepped up next to Sharon, in order

to address the leader. "Beatrice. She is the one who convinced Luke that he wasn't being used to his potential and that he would be better off as an outsider. That was the only reason he was engaging with the other disciples and bringing them into the situation. He didn't feel that way until Beatrice approached him."

"Where is Luke now?" Azril asked.

"The last time I saw him he was with Doris, Janice, Ashley and Justin. They were taking him to change out his uniforms for the light blue. I made the decision that in order for him to get out of isolation early, he would have to start over and go through God's cleanse again," Omegra explained, tears pouring from her eyes.

"This whole situation is getting out of hand. I wonder if Beatrice and Danny have been conspiring with each other for a lot longer than just the past few days. Martin, call for Cory to come in here. As a matter of fact, have him grab Sara and bring her here as well," Azril instructed.

Martin pulled the radio from his belt and called for the tier one head disciples guard. The tier three head disciples guard stood outside waiting for them to arrive.

Omegra wiped the tears from her face with the bottom of her shirt. "Why am I being attacked? I have just sat back and always supported the leader. I know why Beatrice has it out for me, but I'm absolutely confused as to why Danny would have any problems with me."

Azril held his hand out to try and comfort his connected partner the best he could. "Omegra, I understand that you can't control your emotions, but I promise I will take care of everything."

Omegra took a deep breath, sniffed hard and rubbed her eyes. "I trust you Azril and I know that the disciples trust you too. The problem is, some of them don't trust me. Danny believes there are gender roles and I don't want him to convince the rest of the disciples that I am not capable of leading the disciples in the same way you do."

Martin reentered the medical building with Cory, Sara and Danny following behind. "He refused to stay outside."

Everyone in the room turned and stared at Danny. The tier two head disciples guard was trying to keep his connected partner behind him as he stepped up to approach the leader. "What do you want with my connected partner? You should be speaking with me and I will tell her what you want. It is inappropriate for one man to speak to another man's woman. Cory said that you wanted to speak with Sara. I don't know why you went to someone else for *my* connected partner."

"Danny, you were not requested. You are free

to go. I wanted to speak with Sara on a specific matter that doesn't concern you," Azril told him.

"I'm not leaving without Sara," Danny insisted.

Doctor Kyle entered the room after hearing the argument. "There are way too many disciples in here. Anyone the leader doesn't need to speak with needs to leave."

Sharon and Caroline turned and headed out of the building. Omegra stayed in the chair with Martin standing next to her on one side and Farrah standing on the other. Cory, Danny and Sara remained at the foot of the bed. Sara stood with her head down making sure not to make eye contact with anyone.

Azril tried to shift in the bed, in order to sit up. "Hey, Doc. Is there a way that I can make the back of the bed sit up higher? I want to be able to look at the disciples in front of me."

"Absolutely," Kyle said, retrieving the remote for the bed that was tucked into a pocket on the side of the mattress.

Cory and Martin approached the leader and as Kyle pressed the button to position Azril up higher. The two disciples guard helped the leader position his body.

Once Azril was able to look toward the foot of his bed, he only acknowledged one disciple. "Danny, you have been asked to leave. I did not ask for you to be here. I have a particular job assignment for Sara and that is why I requested her."

"No! Your request should go through me. That's it," Danny demanded.

"If that's how you feel," Azril began, gently shrugging his shoulders. "Danny, please pass your radio to Sara. I am putting her in your place as disciples guard for the rest of the month. It was going to only be for a week, but your attitude has changed my decision. You will be placed on morning laundry duty and evening meal duty. Now that has been taken care of, I need to speak to my disciples guard."

Cory and Martin proceeded to escort Danny out of the medical building by grabbing his arms. Danny protested. "Let me go! This isn't right! Men are suppose to be in charge! Women don't have the same authority!"

Cory snatched the walkie talkie off of Danny's waist band as he was shoved out of the building. Cory locked the door in order to keep him from re-entering. The two disciples guard rejoined the others, as Danny banged his fists against the front doors, screaming.

"Thank you. His last statement has solidified the fact that he can no longer be trusted as a disciples guard. Sara, are you willing to take the responsibility of the disciples guard and keep the disciples within the City of Disciples safe?" Azril asked.

"If I take over his position as disciples guard, I would fear for my safety and the safety of my baby," Sara responded.

Azril nodded, acknowledging their ten month old son. "If I could guarantee the safety of both of you, would you be willing to accept the position?"

Sara straightened her posture and stood with both of her hands straight down by her sides. "I would be honored to serve you as part of your disciples guard."

Twenty

As the leader went over what was expected from Sara as a disciples guard, Omegra made eye contact with Kyle, who was standing on the other side of Azril's bed. She was breathing heavily and rubbing her pregnant belly.

Farrah looked down at her and noticed she seemed uncomfortable. "What's happening? Are you okay?"

"I think I'm in labor," Omegra said calmly, before screaming as a contraction spiked.

Kyle moved around the bed and approached Omegra to help her out of the chair. "Let's get you into a bed. I think this is it. Azril, I'm going to get her hooked up and check on the baby. I will send Gayle in to check on you in a few minutes."

"Martin and Farrah need to stay with her," Azril said, motioning for them to follow.

The leader slammed his fist into the mattress he was laying on. This was something they had been waiting for and he was upset that he was going to miss it.

"She's definitely in labor. The doctor wants me to see how you feel about trying to stand up and moving to a wheelchair, so you can be there for the birth of your first child," Gayle told him, as she lowered one side bedrail.

Cory stepped up next to the nurse to assist her in anyway she would need. She put her arms out for Azril to use as leverage. Sara moved around to the other side of the bed and placed her hands against the leader's back, just to help guide him.

"Okay Omegra, do you know how far apart your contractions are?" Doctor Kyle asked, as she leaned back into the bed and he wrapped the fetal monitor around her belly.

"They are about three to five minutes apart. It started last night, but they weren't too strong. Just within the last hour while we were sitting with Azril did they become extremely painful," Omegra told him.

"Why didn't you say something? We have been running around all day and you never once let on that you were in labor," Martin said, interlacing his fingers on the top of his head.

Omegra reached out and tugged on Martin's shirt, pulling him down to get closer to her. "It's my first baby. This could have taken forever if we came in here this morning. The contractions weren't close enough together this morning. Doctor Kyle would have kicked me out."

Doctor Kyle nodded, as he administered an IV. "She's right. There would have been no reason for her to just lay in here all day long. As a matter of fact, since y'all have been walking around all day, it probably helped move the labor along. I'm sure that she will deliver before midnight. If she just laid here all day, she could have been in labor for several days."

Martin took a deep breath and straightened his stance. "I just want to make sure I didn't mess up and potentially harm Omegra, or the baby by not noticing that she was in labor."

"The only way you would have known is if you

knew that every time I rubbed my belly I was having a contraction," Omegra reassured him.

"Okay, the two of you can go. Azril should be wheeled in here at any moment and we don't want the room to be too crowded," Kyle told Martin and Farrah.

"No, Martin and Farrah are here for Omegra and the baby. Martin is the disciples guard for my connected partner and Farrah is the disciples guard for the baby. They are not to go anywhere," Azril informed, as Gayle pushed him into the room.

"Okay, then can they at least wait in the other room? This could get very messy and it's better for the baby to come into the world in a calm and quiet environment," Kyle told them.

"I can understand that. Sara, keep an eye on the door with Cory. Don't let anyone in unless it's a medical emergency," Azril told him, before shifting his entire body toward Farrah and Martin. "Farrah, you and Martin can guard the delivery room and don't let anyone in."

"Whatever you need great leader," Farrah agreed.

Cory and Sara headed out of the building, as Martin and his connected partner exited the room and took their assigned posts.

Gayle closed the door to the labor room as

C. L. Conolly

Doctor Kyle positioned a chair between her legs, to assist Omegra to deliver the first child of the leader. Omegra's water broke as the doctor was checking to see how dilated her cervix was. The contractions became unbearable for her and she was begging for an epidural.

"Omegra, we talked about this. We don't want to drug the baby. An epidural is not an option as long as you can deliver the baby naturally," Azril told her.

"Then hurry up and get it out!" Omegra screamed at him.

"Okay Omegra, you are fully dilated. Go ahead and start pushing. This baby is ready to make their appearance into the City of Disciples," Kyle told her.

The leader's connected partner pushed for about an hour and a half, before they welcomed their new little girl to the City of Disciples. After Azril assisted with cutting the umbilical cord, Doctor Kyle passed the baby to Nurse Gayle, in order to clean off the amniotic fluid.

"She's absolutely beautiful, Omegra," Gayle told her, diapering the newborn.

"If she looks anything like the leader, I'm sure she is gorgeous," Omegra said, as Kyle cleaned her up.

Gayle weighed and measured the baby. "Born

at eleven thirty seven P.M., at seventeen and three quarter inches long. Five pounds, six ounces."

"Oh, she's a tiny baby," Omegra said.

"Is she healthy?" Azril asked, listening to the baby scream.

"She's doing great. Possibly hungry," Gayle said, as she swaddled the baby and walked her over to Omegra.

The leader's connected partner began breast feeding, as Kyle finished cleaning her birth canal. Omegra cried as the baby calmed and latched on to eat.

"Are those happy tears?" Azril asked her.

"We haven't chosen a name yet," Omegra said, switching from happy to sad.

"You pick something you like and I am okay with whatever you decide," Azril told her.

Omegra sniffed hard. "Are you sure?"

"Absolutely," Azril said, slowly lifting his arm and placing his hand on her shoulder.

"How do you feel about Alpha? She is the first baby to the great leader of the disciples," Omegra suggested.

Azril moved his hand down her arm and was able to get ahold of her hand. Interlacing his fingers with hers and kissing the back of her hand. "Alpha is perfect."

"The baby seems to be latching pretty well.

We will keep you here throughout the night, just for observation. If you would like to send Farrah in for instruction, we can inform her on the best way to assist Omegra with taking care of the baby at home," Kyle informed the leader.

Azril agreed and Gayle opened the door in order for Farrah to enter the room. She stood up next to the bed and peered down at the baby cradled in Omegra's arms. The leader leaned back in the wheelchair as the pain from holding his own head up became unbearable.

Gayle noticed the agony on his face. She walked over and crouched down next to him. "Do you need to go back and lay down?"

"I don't want to leave Omegra and Alpha," he told the nurse.

"Go lay down. We are going to be okay. Alpha is sleeping and I will be joining her soon," Omegra told him.

"Okay, Farrah stay here with them. I need to speak with Martin anyway," Azril said, as Gayle wheeled him back to the other room.

Azril gently settled himself back into the bed, as Martin entered the room. "Just the disciple I wanted to see."

"I hope Farrah is okay in there with Omegra," Martin said, sitting down in the chair next to the bed.

"She's doing great. As a matter of fact, she was swooning over the baby when I left," Azril told him. "Is there more to why you're concerned?"

Martin looked down at his hands resting in his lap. "As more of the disciples have become pregnant, Farrah has mentioned wanting a baby. However, due to our circumstance we aren't able to do that. We have had several conversations about adoption, but Farrah has talked about wanting a child of her own."

"How about we set her up as our nanny. She can take care of our children and help Omegra with anything she needs. She can spend everyday with Omegra and Alpha, but still be able to leave without having to deal with all the crying and exhaustion," Azril suggested.

Martin took a deep, overwhelmed breath. "We can talk to her about it and see how Farrah feels about that. The two of us had agreed that we never wanted children. I knew that when I started taking hormone therapy it could cause infertility. I was okay with it and have been taking testosterone for several years in order to transition. I don't know if Farrah was told that her taking estrogen would cause infertility and she was a little upset when I told her that I was uncomfortable with carrying a child. It was not something I ever wanted to do. She is also fully aware that she does not possess the proper organs in order to incubate a baby."

Azril slowly reached out and placed his hand on top of Martin's head for a blessing. "If her being our nanny isn't enough to help her get over her need for her own child, I will see what I can do about possibly helping y'all with adoption if you're okay with that."

Martin closed his eyes, as he felt his entire body relax. "That would be great. Thank you, Leader."

Twenty One

The next morning Omegra and Alpha were cleared to leave the medical center. Farrah assisted with wheeling her over to the room with Azril. Martin took the wheelchair to the back of the medical center, as Omegra moved to the chair next to the bed. Farrah passed the baby to the leader, allowing him to hold his daughter for the first time since her birth.

"Farrah, how would you feel about being our personal nanny. You will be assigned to come to our housing quarters every day and help Omegra with the baby and any other children we may have. You will basically be the disciples guard to the leader's children and assist the leader's connected partner with changing diapers, bottle feedings when that transition happens and anything else that Omegra may need you to do. Are you okay with that?" Azril asked her.

"That would be amazing. Thank you great leader," Farrah said, in a soft, but excited tone.

Alpha had fallen asleep in his arms, so he passed her back to Farrah. She sang several different lullabies to her in a soft, sweet tone, rocking side to side and gazing at the baby in a loving way. Omegra liked the idea of getting help with the children and felt as though Farrah was the perfect fit.

Omegra began dozing off in the chair, just as the baby started getting fussy. "I'm sure she needs to be fed again."

Farrah handed the baby to Omegra. She began to nurse Alpha and did everything to stay awake. "So, tell me who is in charge of what."

"Cory and Sara are taking over the head disciples guard positions. Cory is still tier one head disciples guard, but Sara is taking over tier two head disciples guard until further notice. Martin is still to be your personal guard, like always, as the head disciples guard from tier three. Farrah is technically being promoted to a head disciples guard position, but within tier three with her connected partner. She is to be the personal guard for Alpha and any other children we have," Azril explained.

Omegra switched Alpha to the other side to continue to nurse. "That sounds like a good idea. However, what about Danny?"

"That is what Martin and Farrah are for. They are to keep you and the baby safe. Cory and Sara have also been informed that if Danny tries to use his status to get out of the job duties he has been assigned to, he is to be placed in isolation," Azril told her.

"Since the baby is here now, am I going to continue leading the worship services, or is someone else going to do that?" Omegra asked, closing her shirt and handing the baby back to Farrah.

"I have put Cory in charge of the worship service. I was talking to Gayle about the feeding schedule of the baby and she said that newborns being breast fed can potentially eat every five minutes, or be satisfied for an hour. I don't think it would be fair to you if you were standing in front of all the disciples and having Alpha hanging from your chest," Azril told her, as Martin reappeared.

Omegra stood up. "Thank you. I would however, like to speak with Cory and make sure his message is on the same page as the Disciples Doctrine."

"I have spoken to him and trust him with the worship service. I also told him that he doesn't have to get approval first, but I did tell Sara that if she felt as though his message wasn't in line with the Disciples Doctrine then she was to inform either me, or you," he said.

Omegra kissed Azril on his cheek, then yawned. "Okay, no problem. I'm going to go to the residency building and try to get some sleep. Alpha is on a fifteen to thirty minute feeding schedule, so I haven't slept. Every time I doze off, she's awake to eat again."

Azril smiled. "I hope both of you have sweet dreams. Martin, can you hang back for a moment. I sent Cory and Sara to my office in order to prepare for the worship service tonight."

Martin kissed Farrah on her cheek before he sat down in the chair next to the leader's bedside. "Absolutely, Leader."

"When you feel comfortable, you could start pumping, so I could feed her while you sleep," Farrah suggested, as she exited the medical building directly behind Omegra.

"That could be a while," Omegra told her. "I would like to be able to use breast feeding as bonding time with the baby. As a matter of fact, until I can get a full night's sleep, you will be with her as long as she isn't attached to me."

Farrah smiled as she rubbed one finger across the baby's forehead. "I'm okay with that."

Farrah and the leader's connected partner walked through the property, toward the residency building and every disciple they passed swooned over the baby. Farrah was being super over pro-tective anytime someone would reach out and try to touch the baby. She would hunch over and block them from getting too close.

Omegra rubbed her eyes and barely heard anything anyone said. She was glad when they made it into the office, because that meant she was closer to sleep. Cory was sitting behind the desk writing notes for the evening worship service and Sara was sitting in one of the chairs across from him. Omegra had barely made it up two steps when they heard a kerfuffle coming from just outside the office door. A familiar voice was scolding several others.

Omegra turned and looked at Cory. "That's Danny's voice. What is happening now?"

Cory popped up out of the chair and darted

toward the door, yanking it open. They couldn't believe what they were seeing on the stage in the worship center. Omegra told Farrah to continue up the stairs with the baby.

"Danny, what is going on here?" Cory asked.

Danny had a disciple in a headlock and was waving his butterfly knife around at several other disciples as to hold them off. The disciples being threatened with the knife were trying to deescalate the situation with Danny, pleading with him to release the other disciple. The look on his face appeared as though he was losing his grip on reality.

"These disciples all need to be isolated. They are being defiant toward the chain of command and do not respect the disciples guard," Danny spat, speaking so fast they could barely understand what he said.

"Danny, let go of the disciple. The leader has already had this conversation with you. Please come into the office. This is unacceptable behavior," Cory calmly negotiated.

"This is fucking ridiculous! I'm tired of being disrespected by these assholes who refuse to go through the proper chain of command!" Danny yelled, maneuvering the knife to the disciples neck he was holding on to.

"Danny, that is not the type of language God

approves. Please refrain yourself," Omegra scolded.

"Fuck that! I am a disciples guard! I deserve just as much respect as the leader," Danny said, just as Martin entered the worship center.

"Danny, please put down the knife. This is not the way to handle this. Let's go into the office and talk," Omegra tried.

As Danny yelled, Cory approached Martin to give him a run down of the situation. "I don't want to talk! These disciples need to be isolated and shunned! They don't know how to respect the chain of command!" He turned his back to Cory and Martin in order to face Omegra.

She nodded in order to affirm that Cory and Martin should grab Danny. They had been slowly stepping toward him, so as not to startle him in any way. After she nodded, their steps quickened and they were right behind him within seconds.

"Now Danny, why don't you tell me why you think these disciples should be isolated and shunned." Omegra spoke with understanding.

Just as Danny's hand, which was holding the knife, dropped to his side, Cory and Martin took action. Martin grabbed the knife and the disciple, as Cory interlocked his elbows with Danny's elbows from behind him. The disciple that was being threatened by Danny was freed and returned to the group of disciple witnesses.

"What the fuck is this?" Danny protested.

"Take him down to isolation room one and lock him up," Omegra told Cory and Martin, handing Martin the key to the isolation rooms.

"This is not how this situation is supposed to go. Cory come on, you know me. Let me go. Let me go!" Danny said, as he was ushered into the office.

"Who can tell me what happened?" Omegra asked, addressing the disciples, as she sat down on the chair still in front of the podium.

"Danny spotted us walking into the worship center. When he approached us, he asked why we weren't at our job assignments. I tried to explain that we had some questions about the Disciples Doctrine that we wanted to speak to the leader about. That's when he told us that we had to set up a meeting with the disciple who recruited us and they would go to the disciples guard that was the head of the group who would then set up the meeting with you," one disciple explained.

"We tried to tell him that you said at last night's worship service that we could come to you with any questions we had about the Disciples Doctrine or our safety in the City of Disciples, but that's when he grabbed me and pulled out his knife," the hostage disciple told her.

"He kept yelling about chain of command and how you were too busy to talk to us," a third disciple told the leader's connected partner.

Omegra did her best to stifle a yawn before responding. "Well, I will tell you this, last night I gave birth to the leader's first child. Danny is being placed in isolation in order to avoid this situation from happening again. Cory will be in charge of the worship service until the leader has recovered enough to be released from the medical center. If you still have any questions after tonight's worship service, all you have to do is approach Cory, or Sara and let either of them know you would like to speak with them. Either of them should be able to answer your questions, or ease your concerns. If you feel as though you would rather speak with me, just let them know and they will set up a meeting with me. With the new baby, I don't know how often I'm going to be awake."

"Thank you, Omegra. We appreciate your understanding," the hostage disciple said, before they all turned to leave.

Omegra was relieved she was able to finally go upstairs to her housing quarters. She wasn't sure how much longer she was going to be able to keep her eyes open.

Twenty Two

Martin opened the first isolation room and Cory shoved Danny as hard as he could. Danny fell to the floor and Martin slammed the door closed and locked it. The two disciples guards smiled at each other before they headed back upstairs and into the office.

"Who is at the medical center with the leader?" Cory asked Martin.

"Lawerence ran over and told us about the situation and the leader requested that I come over to see if you needed any assistance. Lawerence stayed behind," Martin explained.

Cory raised his eyebrows. "Okay. Seems like Lawerence is proving himself to be a loyal disciple. Sara, you want to go with me? We should go give the leader an update."

Sara smiled and straightened her stance. "Absolutely. Thank you, Cory."

Martin saluted Cory with two fingers against his forehead, as Cory and Sara headed out to the medical building. Martin headed upstairs to stand guard outside of the leader's living quarters.

Azril saw them as they approached the bed. "Alright Cory, tell me what happened with Danny."

"Danny threatened a group of disciples with a knife and Martin helped me contain him in isolation," Cory said.

Azril shifted, trying to get comfortable. "I'm glad I made the decision to put Sara in his position as disciples guard. How did he react when y'all took him into isolation?"

"He's pretty irate. He was talking about how the disciples guard is just as important as the leader and we should all be treated with the same respect," Cory told him.

"How do y'all feel about that? Do you believe

C. L. Conolly

that the disciples should treat you with as much respect as they show both me and my connected partner?" Azril asked them.

"We are at the mercy of the leader, the one who was chosen by God to lead us to the promised land. The disciples guard is the same as the disciples. We have to give them respect in order to get respect from them," Cory said.

"Sounds as though you understand your place. What about you two, Sara and Lawerence? How do y'all feel about what Danny said?" Azril asked.

Sara placed her hands against her lower back and stood up straight. "I am here to serve you and your connected partner. That is my place. You have been chosen to give us the message of God, so we will have a place in the promised land when we are released from the physical land. Respect is something that's earned, not demanded and anyone who is being disrespectful doesn't deserve the respect of others around them."

Lawerence sat up straight, from the slouching position in the chair next to the leader. "My place is to assist the leader in making sure that all the disciples are safe inside the City of Disciples."

"Good, I appreciate your loyalty. Thank you. Cory, I would like for you to bring the other disciples guard here to me. I want to make sure the others also know their place. However, Martin is exempt from the meeting since I have already spoken to him about this subject and he is keeping my connected partner and newborn safe. Also, if one of you could go check on Danny as well. I don't want him to trash the isolation room," Azril informed.

Cory and Lawerence headed out to gather the other disciples guard, leaving Sara behind to stay with the Leader. Doctor Kyle entered to check on Azril's pain. He had closed his eyes and groaned, not being able to get into a comfortable position.

"Is everything okay, Leader?" Kyle asked.

"When can I get out of here? I feel as though I'm losing control of the disciples," Azril responded.

"In a couple of days, Gayle and I will get you up and moving around. We don't want your muscles to atrophy. The more activity you are able to engage in, the sooner you can be released," Kyle informed.

Meanwhile at the residency building, Cory decided he would go check on Danny, while Lawerence assembled the rest of the disciples guard. He walked upstairs to get the key to isolation from Martin and tell him about the conversation with the leader.

Martin smiled. "It feels good to hear that the

leader of the disciples knows how loyal I am."

Cory playfully nudged Martin's shoulder with his fist. "Are you blushing, Martin?"

"Shut up and go do your job," Martin said, rubbing the palms of his hands against his cheeks, smiling.

Cory headed down to the office, unlocked and opened the isolation hatch, then stepped up to isolation room one. He peered into the small six inch by six inch peep window. Danny had pulled the pillow, sheets and blanket off the bed and flipped the mattress off the bed frame. Luckily the bed frame was bolted to the floor.

The head disciples guard didn't want to open the door, just in case the disciple chose to rush him. He knocked on the window. "Danny, what are you doing?"

Danny stepped up to the door and glared out at Cory, wild-eyed. "This is bullshit, Cory and you know it! Your priorities are all skewed! If you continue to allow the disciples to treat the disciples guard in this way, they will rebel against the leader."

Cory took a deep breath, closed and locked the peep door, then headed up to the office. It wasn't long before Lawerence arrived with the disciples guard. Cory chose to tell those that didn't already know about Sara taking over Danny's place as disciples guard. Most of them exchanged glances and shrugged.

"The leader had a good reason for making the change. I like Sara better than Danny anyway," Jerry said, laughing.

Cory placed his hands, palms together, against his breast bone. "I know the leader will appreciate your approval. The leader has requested a meeting with his disciples guard in order to determine loyalty to the City of Disciples. Before we head over to the medical center, I would just like to inform everyone that the leader may not look like he is in good shape, but he is in good spirits. Please keep your over the top reactions to a minimum."

A couple of the disciples guard seemed apprehensive over the idea about Sara being in the group. Tom and Walter leaned toward each other and whispered.

"I understand how strange this must be as the rest of you are masculine disciples guard and Sara is the first feminine disciples guard of the disciples. However, the leader asked if she would take over for Danny due to his erratic behavior lately," Cory explained.

"Do you feel that she is confident enough to take over for Danny if he would have to be shunned? I know the two of them have a little boy together," Sean asked Cory.

"Let's go ask her. She is at the medical center with the leader and I know she would have no problem explaining her feelings for Danny," Cory said, leading the disciples guard through the property.

Sara was waiting outside the doors of the medical building as they approached. "The leader is asleep. I came out here to wait for y'all to arrive."

Sean stepped up to stand in front of her. "How would you feel if Danny had to be shunned?"

"He has been unraveling lately. Danny told me that he thinks he should be the leader of the disciples because the rest of you are not worthy. He feels that the leader isn't the right leader and he is a false prophet. The decision the leader makes as to his fate, is one that is chosen by God as spoken through Him," Sara said.

"Is that good enough for all of you, or does anyone else have anything negative to say about Azril as the leader of the City of Disciples?" Cory asked the disciples guard.

All nine of the disciples guard who were standing in front of Cory all shook their heads before he led them inside the medical center. They circled around the leader's bed with Cory being at the head of the bed on one side and Lawerence on the other.

Azril had his eyes closed as the disciples guard approached him, but he was aware they were there. "Thank you for joining me here. I want to make sure that each of you make Sara feel welcome as a new disciples guard. I can understand if any of you have questions about the integrity of the disciples guard with the new assignment, but the safety of the disciples has been brought to my attention.

"Assigning Sara to Danny's spot is my way of removing the threat to the disciples and giving the disciples guard a softer expectation. With all of the disciples guard being masculine, some of the disciples find you as being aggressive. As a matter of fact, one of the disciples told me that the only disciples guard they were willing to take their concerns to were either Cory or Martin. If neither of them were available, they would try to find Omegra or just ignore the issue.

"I never want the disciples to feel unsafe and with Danny's behavior lately, that is exactly what is happening. He is being threatening, not just toward the disciples, but also toward his connected partner, his infant son and me. Who's to say that he doesn't turn on the disciples guard, as his way of believing that none of you are worthy?"

"We should be accepting the leader's decision. He is the one God has chosen to lead the disciples and if he feels as though this is the way to keep us all safe, I will accept Sara as part of the disciples guard," Warren announced.

As the rest of the disciples guard murmured in agreement, Azril continued. "I appreciate that all of you are compliant. I need the twelve of you to take charge and keep the disciples safe while I'm here. Cory will be taking over the worship service. My daughter, Alpha, was born this morning and Farrah has been appointed as the personal disciples guard to our children.

"I feel as though the shunning ceremony has caused some of the disciples to feel unsafe in the City of Disciples. As such, outsiders are no longer to be shunned. We are to contact the police to have them removed for trespassing. Also, any shunning scheduled for disciples are to be placed on hold for now.

"Tom and Walter, I would like the two of you to set fire to the shunning pit and allow the fire to burn itself out. Toss in some of the disciples garbage on top. Once the fire burns out, cover the pit with dirt, along with planting a bush in its place. All shunning ceremonies are on hold for the time being.

"As well, seeing as there are an abundance of young children here in the City of Disciples, we are going to need to appoint some disciples as not only teachers, but also childcare services. Warren, Tom and Walter, do you think that your connected partners Jessica, Katie and Sharon would be willing to assist Farrah and Omegra with the disciple children?"

"I'm sure that Katie would be willing to teach the disciple children," Tom said.

"I can assure you that Jessica will do what is requested of her for the City of Disciples," Warren told the leader.

"I don't know if Sharon would want to give up her permanent job assignment as meal service, but I can ask if she would watch the kids," Walter said.

"If you aren't sure, I can always ask someone else. Lawrence, what about Samantha?" Azril asked, deciding to move on and keep his eye on Walter.

"Samantha would be honored," Lawerence agreed without hesitation.

"Thank you Tom, Warren and Lawerence. Sara, could you please round up Katie, Jessica, Samantha, as well as Sharon so I may speak with them. The rest of you are dismissed. Go back to your guard posts," Azril instructed.

Twenty Three

Cory stayed behind, as his post was technically to guard the leader. "I will speak with Walter and find out why he hesitated when you requested his connected partner. That response seemed unusual for him."

"Thank you, Cory. You have been a loyal disciple from the beginning. I thought Danny was too, but now I seem to have my guard up for anyone who hesitates when I make a request," Azril responded.

Sara returned, followed by the four disciples the leader requested to meet with. Cory stepped out of the medical building and stood outside the front doors, as the five disciples stood in front of the bed, waiting for instruction.

Azril motioned to the chair next to the bed. "Sharon, please have a seat. Sara, could you please find Nurse Gayle and see if the other three disciples could also get chairs."

Sharon hesitantly sat down. "Did I do something wrong, sir?"

"Are you happy here?" Azril asked her.

Tilting her head, she furrowed her brow. "Of course I am. I love being a Disciple of God. You saved me from an abusive relationship."

"Your connected partner Walter, doesn't seem to think that you would be willing to follow instruction given to you by me," the leader informed her.

Sharon crossed her hands, placing both of them flat on her chest. "I absolutely would follow any instructions that came from you. You are my leader."

"When I asked him if you would be willing to assist with taking care of the City of Disciples children, whether it be as a teacher or for childcare, he expressed to me that you would not do

C. L. Conolly

that," he said.

Tears formed in Sharon's eyes. "He never even asked me. If the request came from you, Omegra, or any of the disciples guard, I would definitely do what was asked of me."

"I'm glad to hear that. What if I told you that due to his defiance, Walter could be facing possible isolation?" Azril wondered.

Sharon lowered her head and looked down at her lap. "Whatever you think is necessary, Leader."

"My next question is, if Walter were to be isolated, would you be willing to move into his position of disciples guard?" the leader asked her.

Sharon raised her head. "I would be honored."

Sara and Gayle returned with three other chairs for Samantha, Katie and Jessica. They joined Sharon next to the leader's bed.

Azril finally opened his eyes. "Thank you Sara and Gayle. Sara, you can join Cory outside on post. You are to shadow Cory until we are sure that the other disciples guard have accepted you within their ranks."

Sara headed out of the medical center and joined Cory. "I'm guessing we are keeping an eye out for Walter."

Cory turned his head and looked at his new disciples guard partner. "Yes. The leader is afraid that Walter could be displaying the same demeanor as Danny. I don't feel comfortable discussing Danny with you though."

Sara was confused. Danny was only Cory's friend, but he was *her* connected partner. "I understand, but he wasn't exactly the same person I had met when the City of Disciples had first assembled. After we were connected, any time we were alone, he was very controlling. After our son was born, he tried to teach our son that he was to order me to do things for him because it didn't matter how old he was, in his first year he is still a man and above any woman."

Cory rubbed his face with his hands in frustration. "If the defiance of the disciples guard continues, the disciples could lose faith in the leader's ability to lead them."

Walter walked up to the medical center. "I want to speak with the leader."

"You'll have to wait. He's in there giving instruction to several disciples," Sara informed him, asserting her new position.

"Okay, so can one of you announce to the leader that I'm here?" Walter asked.

"Why? Are you afraid that the leader is upset with you?" Cory asked.

"I feel like I crossed the line by not just agreeing with the leader when it was requested for

Sharon to change her job assignment," Walter admitted.

Cory looked down at his feet and sighed, before he pivoted and headed inside the building. To ensure that Walter waited to be summoned, The tier one head disciples guard locked the door behind him.

"Leader, Walter has arrived and would like to speak with you," Cory informed.

"Send him in. I'm almost done here," Azril told Cory, turning back to the disciples. "Okay, Gayle is suppose to be getting me up and moving around in a couple of days. I'm going to try and meet with the four of you again soon. Decide what your strong suits are to teach the children, then meet with Farrah in the morning to ensure your job assignments."

Cory waited until they were heading out of the medical center before he unlocked the door and allowed Walter to enter.

He stopped his connected partner as they passed each other in the front waiting area. "Hey, Sharon. I'm sorry I didn't recommend you when the leader asked."

"The disciples have been dismissed. Walter, please have a seat. And could one of you please let Cory know I need him to come in here as well," Azril requested.

Samantha, Sharon, Jessica and Katie lowered their heads and walked out of the medical center. Samantha indicated that the leader wanted to see Cory by tilting her head. He nodded, then went inside.

Cory stepped up to the foot of the bed. "Leader, you wanted to see me?"

"I need you to take Walter down into the isolation area," Azril said, making eye contact with Cory.

Walter whipped his head back and forth between Azril and Cory. "Why am I going to isolation? Leader, I'm sorry. I... it's not that I didn't think that Sharon couldn't do the job, I just know how much she enjoys her job assignment."

"Walter, your response to my request earlier was unexpected. I spoke to Sharon and she said that she would be honored to assist with watching and teaching the disciple children. It seems as though you are the one defying my order," Azril told him.

"I'm sorry, sir. Please give me a chance. I promise my thoughts are only on the message in the Disciples Doctrine and not those of Danny. I don't understand what happened," Walter begged.

"You will understand when you end up being the next isolated disciple, right next to Danny,"

Azril said, as Cory grabbed Walter.

"Please, Leader. I will do anything to continue being part of your disciples guard. If you require private worship sessions, I will come here several times a day to meet with you," Walter continued.

"Okay Cory, let him go. But please tell me what you were thinking when you rejected my request," Azril asked.

Walter took a deep breath. "I just feel like I don't have the right to make decisions for my connected partner. I would have to ask her and she would have to agree before I could give you the affirmative."

The leader placed his hand against the immobility brace. "I don't know why you didn't just say that in the first place. I would have respected you more for that answer and my response wouldn't have been so harsh. Now, I'm going to allow you to do a disciples guard job duty for me, but Cory or Lawerence will need to go with you."

"I'm willing to do anything. What can I do for you?" Walter responded.

"I need someone to get Beatrice and bring her here. The disciples guard who brings her here must be willing to contain her and keep her from putting her hands on me, or getting too close," the leader instructed.

"I will take him down there to retrieve Beatrice

and bring them both back here. I will make sure everything is within compliance of the City of Disciples," Cory obliged with the leader.

Cory and Walter headed out of the medical center. Azril relaxed into the bed and closed his eyes again, preparing himself for the interaction he was going to have with Beatrice.

Twenty Four

Cory led Walter back to the residency building, leaving Sara behind to stay with the leader. The head disciples guard descended the stairs first, followed by the tier six disciples guard, down into the isolation area. Cory decided to peep in at Danny first.

Danny had his face pressed up against the peep window, as if he knew Cory would come back. He slammed his forehead into the polycarbonate glass panel and screamed. "Fuck you, Cory! I'm not speaking to anyone except the leader! Leave me alone!"

"Is that what is happening right now?" Walter asked.

Cory closed and locked the peep window for isolation room one and walked toward room ten. "Now you see why the leader wasn't happy with your defiance."

Walter rolled his eyes. "I wasn't defying the leader of the disciples. I wanted to ask Sharon first. Like I said, she has her own thoughts and can make decisions on her own. I didn't think it was my place to answer for her."

Cory placed his hand on Walter's shoulder. "That was the problem. You didn't explain that to the leader. He would have been more understanding. Danny has shown that he doesn't believe that the disciples were all created equal."

"It was not my intention to make the leader feel as though I was being defiant. I feel that all disciples were created equal by God and I don't have the right to speak for my connected partner," Walter said.

Cory patted Walter on his back. "I'm glad to hear that. I will make sure to have the leader bring it to the attention of Sharon as well. I saw the way she reacted to you when you went in to speak with the leader. That means he asked her if she would be willing to take over your place in the disciples guard if you were to be placed in isolation."

Walter lowered his head. "I hope to get this cleared up. Danny has never given off the indication that he didn't agree that everyone was created equal. I'm confused as to how the leader came to the conclusion that Danny doesn't believe we are all equal."

Cory sighed heavily. "I will tell you, but this stays between us, as disciples guards. The rest of the City of Disciples don't need to know."

Walter nodded, vehemently. "Absolutely."

Cory directed Walter into a cubby in the back of the isolation area. "Danny was initially upset that Omegra took over the worship service. He felt that she wasn't qualified to run the City of Disciples. He said that he should be the one to take over until the leader was able to return to his position because women are not able to lead the same as men."

Walter furrowed his eyebrows and tilted his head. "That is completely against the entire message of the Disciples Doctrine. The disciples are feminine or masculine, but everyone is equal. Also, the leader could be either feminine or masculine as long as the disciples respect their authority."

Cory raised his eyebrows and pulled his lips into his mouth, nodding. "I'm glad that you understand that. Now we have to deal with the one who doesn't know how boundaries work."

The head disciples guard walked over and stepped up to the door to room ten. Walter was close by preparing himself for the disciple inside to fight. As he slid the key into the lock Cory looked over at Walter and nodded his head. He turned the key and opened the door.

Beatrice was sitting on the bed, with her legs crossed, eyes closed and her back against the wall. "Where is Azril? I'm not speaking to anyone except Azril."

Cory rubbed his forehead with frustration. "Beatrice, I know you have been told before that it is disrespectful to refer to the leader by his first name. Also, the leader is in the medical center recovering from an injury. You know that. However, he has requested to speak with you. We are here to take you to him."

Beatrice's eyes popped open, as she bounced up quickly off the bed. "Oh, why didn't you say so. Let's go."

Beatrice tried pushing passed Cory as she stepped out of the room. However, Cory grabbed her arm and stopped her from getting too far. He pulled a couple of zip ties out of his pocket and cuffed her hands behind her back.

"Wait! Why are you going to parade me through the City of Disciples like a criminal?" Beatrice yelled.

"You don't know how to control yourself around the leader. Calling him by his name and not by his title of leader, shows that you don't respect him as the leader. As such, you are classified as a criminal within the City of Disciples. The disciples know that the things you have said are inappropriate and none of them are going to think twice about you being dragged through the property with restraints on," Cory explained.

"I'm done speaking with you. Let's just go," Beatrice said, looking straight ahead.

Cory and Walter walked her through the property to the medical building. Azril was asleep when they approached his bed.

"Oh, Azril. It pains me to see you like this," Beatrice squawked.

Azril startled awake, opening his eyes. "Good grief, Beatrice. Lower your voice. There is no reason for you to be screaming in here."

"Tell them to let me go," she told him, still with a raised voice, but quieter than before.

"Look, if you can't calm down and listen, I'm

going to have them take you back to isolation," the leader told her. "Sit down."

Cory forced her into the chair next to the bed. Both Walter and Cory stood on each side of her, with one of their hands on each one of her shoulders to keep her in the chair.

Beatrice took a deep breath, before speaking calmly. "Okay, *Leader.* What can I do to get out of isolation? I feel like I have spent more time in isolation, than I have within the disciples."

"Your behavior has been inappropriate ever since you chose to offer yourself to me. As much as I can't trust you, I feel as though you are the perfect disciple for what I need," Azril said.

"I will do anything for you." Beatrice tried to lean forward in the chair to get closer to him, but the two disciples guard held her in place, squeezing her shoulders.

"Danny doesn't see all disciples as being equal. I have had the same thought for you, as you don't feel as though Omegra is worthy to be my connected partner. I want you to go with Lawerence to the isolation and speak with Danny," Azril instructed.

"If you let me go, I will do whatever you want." She curled up one side of her mouth.

"I should be able to meet with you again within the next couple of days. You will be placed in isolation room two, next to Danny. After each meal, Lawerence will come down and allow you to speak with Danny as your work detail. During meal times, you will be locked separately in your rooms," the leader explained.

"But I'm still in isolation?" Beatrice whined.

"If you can get him to change his mindset by the time I am able to return to the residency building, then you can both be released," Azril told her.

Beatrice sighed heavily and rolled her eyes. "Fine. Two days. But what happens if I can't change his mindset in that time?"

Azril smiled. "He will be shunned and I will match you with a disciple that will become your connected partner in order to keep you in line with the message in the Disciples Doctrine."

Beatrice agreed and Azril closed his eyes again. Cory and Walter hooked their elbows under her arms and led her out of the medical center. She was taken back to the isolation and placed in room two to wait until Lawerence came in for her job assignment.

Lawerence waited until after the worship service to go down into the isolation. Cory came down with him, just to take the key back upstairs in order to lock the hatch.

Cory opened both isolation rooms. "The three of you are going to be locked down here. The leader gave me permission to acquire a Glock .45 and I will be up in the office with it. Locked and loaded and ready to send a bullet right between your eyes if anything happens to Lawerence. Do the two of you understand that?"

Both Danny and Beatrice raised their eye brows and nodded. Cory looked over at Lawerence before heading back up into the office and locking the hatch.

Lawerence addressed the two isolated disciples. "I'm going to allow the two of you to go into either one of your isolation rooms and I'm going to sit in the chair at the bottom of the stairs. The door must remain open and I can come over and eavesdrop at any time to tell the leader what the two of you are talking about."

Beatrice giggled. "Whatever, guy. Do what you want."

Lawerence rolled his eyes and walked over to have a seat. Beatrice and Danny decided to go into isolation room two. They smiled slyly at each other, knowing that they were only going to continue their conversation about the two of them taking over as the leaders of the City of Disciples.

About the Author

C. L. Conolly is an avid horror and true crime fan. Her novels are meant to bring attention to real world issues with a major gore focus. She attends several horror conventions and events each year in order to meet readers in person. To find out more, check out www.clconolly.com and follow on all social media platforms.

When C. L. Conolly isn't writing, she's relaxing at her country home with her husband, family and pets. She has one son, a daughter-in-law and two grandchildren.

Facebook - C. L. Conolly - Author
Instagram - C. L. Conolly
Twitter - @CLConolly
TikTok - @c.l.conolly
YouTube - @c.l.conolly

www.ingramcontent.com/pod-product-compliance
Lightning Source LLC
Chambersburg PA
CBHW010302100726
47904CB00011B/2708